WINTER LONGING

Tricia Mills

razOr
bill

RAZORBILL

An Imprint of Penguin Group (USA) Inc.

Winter Longing

RAZORBILL

Published by the Penguin Group
Penguin Young Readers Group
345 Hudson Street, New York, New York 10014, U.S.A.
Penguin Group (USA) Inc., 375 Hudson Street, New York, New York 10014, U.S.A.
Penguin Group (Canada), 90 Eglinton Avenue East, Suite 700, Toronto, Ontario,
Canada M4P 2Y3 (a division of Pearson Penguin Canada Inc.)
Penguin Books Ltd, 80 Strand, London WC2R 0RL, England
Penguin Ireland, 25 St Stephen's Green, Dublin 2, Ireland
(a division of Penguin Books Ltd)
Penguin Group (Australia), 250 Camberwell Road, Camberwell, Victoria 3124,
Australia (a division of Pearson Australia Group Pty Ltd)
Penguin Books India Pvt Ltd, 11 Community Centre,
Panchsheel Park, New Delhi—110 017, India
Penguin Group (NZ), 67 Apollo Drive, Mairangi Bay, Auckland 1311, New Zealand
(a division of Pearson New Zealand Ltd)
Penguin Books (South Africa) (Pty) Ltd, 24 Sturdee Avenue,
Rosebank, Johannesburg 2196, South Africa
Penguin Books Ltd, Registered Offices: 80 Strand, London WC2R 0RL, England

10 9 8 7 6 5 4 3 2 1

Copyright © 2010 Trish Milburn
All rights reserved

Library of Congress Cataloging-in-Publication Data is available

ISBN: 978-1-59514-288-7

Printed in the United States of America

The scanning, uploading and distribution of this book via the Internet or
via any other means without the permission of the publisher is illegal and punishable
by law. Please purchase only authorized electronic editions, and do not participate in
or encourage electronic piracy of copyrighted materials. Your support of the author's
rights is appreciated.

The publisher does not have any control over and does not assume any responsibility
for author or third-party websites or their content.

To those who have brought Alaska to life for me even though I've never been there: novelists Dana Stabenow and Jean Craighead George; the creators of *Northern Exposure* and *Men in Trees*; and the forces behind and the boat crews of *The Deadliest Catch*.

Mrs. Frank, my second-grade teacher, handed me the stack of valentines from my classmates. I noticed that two had the same handwriting on the outside. I opened the first.

"Have a Beary Happy Valentine's Day.

—Spencer"

I glanced at Spencer before opening the second one. He was busy opening his own valentines. When I slid the card out of the envelope, my heart beat a little faster.

"Will you be mine?

—Spencer"

CHAPTER

The drone of a plane engine stopped me in my tracks, and adrenaline surged through my veins. I looked up into the cloudy, midday sky. But what I'd heard wasn't the familiar red-and-black Piper Super Cub carrying my brand-new boyfriend. Instead, it was Harry Logan's yellow Cessna 185, probably returning from Anchorage with another load of supplies for the residents of Tundra.

I turned my gaze toward the Aleutian Mountain Range to the east: low clouds hugged the higher points of the snow-capped, volcanic peaks. Even squinting, I couldn't distinguish a speck of red against the white. I'd been wondering all morning how Spencer's flying test was going. How long before he got back to town? Before he left this morning, did he eat part of the cake I'd baked for him? Had he thought of me and what we'd shared the night before?

My lips warmed at the memory of his soft, sweet lips.

"Good morning, Winter."

Embarrassment filled me when I realized I'd been caught reliving kissing Spencer by Mrs. Kerr, our next-door neighbor, host of today's annual Labor Day cookout and the person

Mom had sent me over to help with the party preparations. She stood in the driveway with a bag of groceries in her arms and a wide smile on her face. Ack! I imagined her being able to read my thoughts, see my steamy memories.

I pushed those thoughts away and took a couple steps forward. "Can I help you with that?"

"I've got this one, but there's one more in the back of the truck."

I breathed a sigh of relief when she headed inside and I didn't have to face her anymore. My memories were mine and mine alone. Oh, okay, so they all got spilled to my best friend, Lindsay, but that was to be expected, right? Like an inherent right of wearing the best-friend label. Equal to being American, meaning you had the right to vote and pursue happiness.

Besides, keeping that much giddiness inside without sharing it might very well do me physical harm. I didn't want to injure myself right as my life had zoomed straight into the fantasticsphere.

Grocery bag in hand, I made my way in the back door to the Kerrs' house, trying to keep my smile with a mind of its own under control.

"Jesse!" Mrs. Kerr called up the stairs just as I walked inside the kitchen. "Come on, sleepyhead." She looked back at me, smiled, and shook her head. "The American male. They could sleep half their lives away if we let them." She took the grocery bag from me and set it on the center island.

I laughed a little, thinking about how Spencer always threatened me with dire consequences if I ever woke him on a weekend day before ten. Of course, he'd get up early for flying and school, but everything else risked at least the stink eye before the magic hour of 10 a.m.

Jesse Kerr, fellow member of the Tundra School senior class and jock extraordinaire, loudly made his way down the stairs. He paused for a moment when he saw me. "Oh, hey, Winter." Then he proceeded toward the fridge.

"Hey." Despite living next door to each other and being in the same class, it always felt a little odd to speak to Jesse. He was friendly enough, but it wasn't like we inhabited the same social circle. I pulled my attention away from him and refocused on his mom. "What can I do? Mom sent me over to help."

"That was nice. Let's see." Mrs. Kerr scanned the kitchen. "I need some snack mix made up, and there are some cupcakes over there that need icing." She pointed toward two trays of cooled cupcakes at the end of the far counter, and I nodded. "Jesse, you help. I'm going to go start setting up things outside."

As soon as his mom stepped outside, Jesse met my gaze. "Run. Run for you life," he said with lots of drama.

I laughed and headed toward the cupcakes. "Not a fan of the annual picnic?"

He shrugged. "It's okay. Mom just goes a little overboard. We end up eating leftovers for a week."

"So I shouldn't tell her I think we need more hot dogs or baked beans?"

He narrowed his dark eyes. "If you do, you might mysteriously fall prey to random snowball attacks this winter."

I gave him my you-don't-scare-me look. "You do realize that can go both ways, right?"

He grinned. "Guess we'll have to see who wins."

I rolled my eyes and started icing cupcakes. Jesse downed the rest of his juice, then pulled the makings for snack mix out of the grocery bags.

"You sound way too chipper this morning," Jesse said after a couple of minutes.

Only when I glanced at him did I realize I'd been whistling. Well, so what? I was happy, and nothing was going to dim that fact.

"I'm in a good mood. Live with it, grumpy boy."

He tossed a pretzel at me, which I dodged with unusual quickness. "Hope you shoot pucks better than that."

My taunt about his hockey prowess prompted him to pitch another pretzel and what looked like a wheat square at me. I grabbed the butter knife coated with icing and ran toward him.

He laughed and ran around the island, just barely eluding me. Each time I thought I was close enough to inflict sticky, sweet payback, he surged just out of reach. When I rounded the island a third time, I screeched to a halt. Patrice Murray, aka Jesse's girlfriend, aka Queen Witch of Tundra School, aka Brunhilda, stood in the doorway with a less-than-attractive glare on her face. I wouldn't have been the least bit surprised if she'd pulled an ice dagger from behind her and gone after me with mean-girl ferocity.

"What's going on here?" she asked.

Jeez, did she have to sound as if she'd found us naked and rolling on the kitchen floor?

"It's commonly called a food fight." *Genius.* I turned my back on her to return to the cupcakes before I made my gagging face.

"Come outside. Everyone's starting to arrive," Patrice said.

I knew she was speaking to Jesse by the way her tone of voice had changed, to sweet with an edge of conniving.

"I need to finish this up," Jesse said.

"Winter can finish in here."

"Patrice—"

"I got it," I said as I looked back at him. "Almost done anyway."

Patrice's face reflected victory. Let her think she'd won. What she didn't know was that I just couldn't stand to listen to her voice anymore. She wasted no time dragging Jesse out the door.

He might be a decently nice guy, but he had amazingly bad taste in the girlfriend department.

I finished icing the last cupcake and tossed the rest of the party mix fixings into the bowl Jesse had started.

"What's up with the snarl on Brunhilda's face?" Lindsay asked from the open doorway.

"I think it had something to do with me being in the same hemisphere as her boyfriend without her permission."

Lindsay snorted. "Did you tell her that you've got better taste than that?"

"No. I don't even want to speak Spencer's name in her evil presence." I lifted the tray of cupcakes and nodded at the bowl of party mix. "Grab that."

We headed outside, where Mr. and Mrs. Kerr were greeting the guests flowing into their backyard, including my parents.

"Cal, Lara, good to see you," Mr. Kerr said to Mom and Dad as Lindsay and I drew near. Judging by his enthusiasm, you'd think they'd traveled from Fairbanks for the cookout instead of from just next door.

He took a step toward us as we placed the cupcakes and party mix on one of the tables. "Lindsay, nice to see you." He shook his head. "Winter, you're certainly turning into a beautiful young lady. You take after your sisters."

Was something in the grill smoke making him high? My dark hair and complexion came from Dad, while the twins' blond beauty was directly linked to Mom's genetics. Not to mention, I'm the odd man out in the practical-career department. Lesa planned to follow in Dad's footsteps and become a doctor so she could tend to the medical needs of some village in the Alaskan bush. Kristen made my kindergarten teacher mom deliriously happy by studying education, though she aimed to teach Alaska history to high schoolers rather than finger painting to munchkins.

Me? My secret desire? I wanted to be a costume designer in Hollywood. Not very practical for a girl from small-town Alaska. At least I could share my dream with Spencer, whose own dream also would take him away from the cocoon of Tundra, of Alaska. I could already imagine him flying all over the world and writing about what he saw. The Bill Bryson of the air.

I smiled and uttered a "thanks" to Mr. Kerr, who (despite being a little dweeby) was a nice guy. I couldn't hear him talk without hearing his radio commercials for Tundra Foods in my head. "Come on in to Tundra Foods! Best grocery prices in town!" Of course, no one could argue with *that* claim, since the Kerrs owned the *only* grocery in Tundra.

Lindsay hooked her arm through mine and guided me into the throng of partygoers. "Since you've dragged me to this, I've decided it's going to serve a very important purpose." She unlinked our arms and rubbed her hands together as she scanned the crowd. "I need a hot date when the Snow Ball rolls around, and this is the perfect place to start looking for the lucky guy."

"O-kay." I looked at Lindsay as if she'd been victim to a body snatching. Since when did she want to scope out Tundra's slim pickings? "This plan came from where?"

"From hearing you go on about your little excursion with Spencer last night. You already have the hot date. I'm not going to be the only loser without one. There's got to be *someone* worthy of action besides Spencer."

I frowned at her, annoyed. I wasn't sure why, but I felt oddly protective of my fledging romance.

She stopped scanning the crowd long enough to glance at me. "Oh, get real. You know I don't like Spencer that way." She snorted. "Ew. That'd be like dating one of my brothers."

I couldn't help it; I'd always been a little jealous of the fact that Lindsay had been friends with Spencer first.

Even though the three of us were now inseparable, they'd still shared memories I'd never been a part of. But he was with me now. A wave of pure giddiness swept through me. I couldn't wait to see him again, kiss him.

Thinking this, I stifled a squeal.

I still couldn't believe I'd snuck out last night. It was a miracle I'd made it all the way to Spencer's house without dropping the cake I'd baked him. I'd almost turned back before working up the guts to knock on his bedroom window, while his parents slept just across the hall. The same jittery feeling I'd felt then made my skin tingle again as I replayed the encounter in my mind for what had to be the thousandth time.

Lindsay punched me on the arm. "I fully expect more details than that pittance you gave me on the phone. So spill! I know you're thinking about it."

I remembered his broad and intimate smile as he'd leaned forward out of his window to reveal his shirtless torso.

"It was amazing."

"So, what did he say when you showed up with a cake in the middle of the night?"

"He teased me, of course. Then I started babbling, saying how it was supposed to be a congratulations cake but I couldn't wait to give it to him, so now it was a good-luck cake. At that point, I pretty much was dying of embarrassment and shoved the cake at him, told him it was carrot cake." His favorite.

He'd taken the lid off and seen the frosted plane. The night air had caused goose bumps to pebble his skin as he leaned on the windowsill and smiled at me. "My sweet, thoughtful girlfriend." He'd lingered on the last word, like he was savoring it.

"And then?" Lindsay prompted, pulling me from my reverie again.

"He reached out and grabbed my hand, pulled me toward him. He said he was glad I'd finally made the first move." I'd asked him to the Snow Ball earlier in the day. It had been one of the scariest, most impulsive things I'd ever done, but also the smartest—it had gotten us to where we were now.

"Really?"

Which was exactly the question I'd asked. "Yeah."

Amy Peterboro, one of Lindsay's teammates on the basketball team, stopped us to ask Lindsay something about the practice schedule. I stared off toward the mountains again, letting myself drift back to the night before, to the moment I'd been telling Lindsay about.

"Really?" My voice had sounded breathless.

"Yes, really," he'd said. His words, cloaked in the surrounding night and full of unspoken promises, sounded extra sexy. Then his expression grew more serious. "I was afraid to risk our friendship."

"Me too!" I said it a little too loudly, immediately embarrassed by my lack of control. Spencer put his finger against my lips, sending a delicious zing racing through me. He glanced back into the darkness of his room, apparently listening. Satisfied, he returned his attention to me. "As much as my parents adore you, I'm not sure they'd be thrilled to see you outside my bedroom window at 1 a.m."

The sense of risk made it all the more intense when he pulled me to him and kissed me, a kiss that was deeper and more heart-pounding than our last. My hands ran over his naked shoulders, and an unexpected urgency coursed through me. I wanted it to go on forever. My fingers trailed along the goose bumps on his chest, and I felt him suppress a shiver.

"You're freezing," I'd said, finally breaking away.

"Funny, I feel pretty warm at the moment." He pulled me back in.

"Hello, Mission Control to Winter."

I glanced at Lindsay and noticed that Amy was gone.

"Sorry. I just can't stop thinking about last night."

"So, is he a good kisser?"

Warmth flooded my face, but I nodded. "Awesome! I've never felt so wonderful in my whole life. Still feel that way today."

"Must be good if even Brunhilda can't ruin your mood." We navigated away from a throng of adults. "So, how late were you there?"

"About one. I finally had to leave so he could get some rest before his test this morning." I glanced up at the sky. "He said he'd take me up for a flight after he got his license."

"Romantic, especially if he lands you in some secluded spot."

I couldn't help the little squeal of joy that escaped me.

"You two are going to be sickly sweet now, aren't you?" Lindsay asked with mock horror.

"Probably." I gifted her with my widest smile. "Linds, I

think he's liked me for a long time, maybe as long as I've liked him."

"Did he say that?"

"No, but when I asked him about those two Valentine's cards from him in second grade, if he'd meant to send me two, he just grinned and said, 'What do you think?'"

Lindsay stopped and looked at me. "How were you even able to sleep after that?"

"I couldn't for a long time. I think I danced all the way home. Then I couldn't help it; I texted him, told him I couldn't stop thinking about him."

"Can't sleep," I'd typed. "Should read. What? *The Tempest* or *Persuasion*?" I'd giggled, pretty sure I knew what his answer would be since he was no great fan of the Bard.

"Did he offer to come over, to help find a way to get you to sleep?" Lindsay's wicked eyebrow wiggle prompted me to shove at her shoulder.

"No! He'd already fallen asleep."

Lindsay turned her attention to the crowd around us. In a small town like ours, *everyone* showed up at parties. "Well, you two will be sucking face for the foreseeable future." She placed her hands on her hips. "I need a man." She sighed. "Okay, a boy will do. So listen, option No. 1: Matthew Stanislowski. Decent looking, reasonably intelligent, but his mom is a bit of a freak." She stretched her face into a look of mock fright. "Brock Robertson." She ticked off option two. "Hands roam too much. Dave Cooney." She shuddered. "No thanks. I'd rather go out with a girl."

I groaned as Lindsay kept up her running commentary of every male classmate she spotted. Much as I loved Lindsay, I couldn't wait for Spencer to hurry back and spirit me away.

"Don't groan at me. I've listened to you go on and on about Spencer for years! You owe me."

"Okay, fine." She had a point. I kept my mouth shut as she continued to prattle. In addition to her unceasing list of pros and cons, other snatches of the conversations around us sailed past me as I floated along on my happy cloud. Quotas for the king and opilio crab seasons, predictions about the upcoming winter, the rising price of groceries, prospects for Tundra School's basketball and hockey teams.

But it was all muffled, hiding behind my eagerness to see Spencer again. To wrap my arms around him, kiss him, snuggle on the couch with him, and have him read to me from the latest Dana Stabenow mystery or hilarious Bill Bryson travelogue. I still had a hard time believing we'd finally moved beyond the friendship barrier. But my long-held dream had, in fact, come gloriously true.

I was so lost in my thoughts of Spencer that I nearly ran into Lindsay. She'd stopped navigating the crowd as abruptly as she'd stopped her monologue. Instead, she stared ahead, stunned.

"*Who* is that?" Her voice sounded breathy.

I peered around Vernon Sibigorski, the enormous mechanic who worked at Patrice Murray's dad's garage. Considering there was only one person in my line of vision whom Lindsay hadn't known for years, it didn't take a lot of deductive reasoning to figure out who she meant. The tall, blond guy a few yards ahead couldn't look any more different from Lindsay's dark Aleut coloring if he tried.

"I take it you haven't met Caleb Moore yet," I said. "He's Mayor Ellis's new stepson."

"Pretty sure I would have remembered him," she said, continuing to stare at Tundra's newest resident. "If they grow them like that in Oregon, I was born in the wrong state." She licked her lips and finally stopped looking at Caleb long enough to wink at me.

Everyone in Tundra knew the story of the mayor's new family. In a town that barely hit the two-thousand population mark—counting those who lived out on remote homesteads—and boasted not a single stoplight, the mayor finding love on the Internet was front-page-caliber news.

"He's okay, I guess," I said, mainly to tease Lindsay. Caleb was, in fact, nice looking. Not in Spencer's league, of course, but then, no one was.

"Okay? He's perfect." Lindsay looked like she might drool on herself. "How did I not know when he arrived in town?"

"He and his mom flew in yesterday—you must have been fishing."

A fishing trip that would help Lindsay's family survive through the winter. I wondered when it would hit her how vastly different her world was from that of Tundra's new first son.

The look of total awe on Lindsay's face worried me. She wasn't typically one to go goggle-eyed for a guy, but maybe that was beginning to change. And even in Alaska, where neighbors banded together for survival, the blond Mr.

Perfect and the daughter of poor natives were an unlikely pair. No matter how you looked at it, Caleb and Lindsay didn't exactly scream "happily ever after."

But she wasn't looking for that, was she? Linds just wanted a date to the Snow Ball. And today, I was inclined to believe in the impossible.

"Maybe you should go welcome him to Tundra." I nudged her in the ribs.

At first, she looked like the very idea frightened her to death. But then she straightened and looked more like the Lindsay I knew and loved. "Not a bad idea. Grab him before someone else snatches him up."

"He's not a sandwich, Linds," I said.

"No, he's yummier." She headed in Caleb's direction.

I hung back, watching, hoping he wasn't a cocky, spoiled, rich boy destined to pulverize her self-esteem. Though she never wallowed in self-pity, she'd gone through enough crap already; and I had the feeling I didn't know the half of it. Despite our long friendship, Lindsay wasn't exactly the open-up-and-share type. Still, the last thing *anyone* needed was a broken heart. And I feared that's what she might get if she set her sights on Caleb.

Part of my fear melted when he noticed her approaching and smiled—a nice, friendly, genuine smile. Hey, maybe this would work out. Wouldn't it be awesome if both of us spent our senior year with wonderful, hot guys? I was in the middle of sighing with relief when I noticed a gaggle of Patrice's acolytes as well as Drew Chernov, aka Biggest Jerk on the Planet, approaching Caleb from another direction.

They reached him first. Lindsay stopped moving, watched as the group guided him away. Anger swept over me when I saw Drew smirk at Lindsay. Not for the first time, I wanted to punch him all the way to Nome. Caleb glanced back at Lindsay, gave her a powerless expression of apology. I just stared. If he wanted to talk to her, why didn't he pull himself away from the leech girls?

Lindsay spun around and walked back toward me. "Dude, I'm so hungry I could eat my arm. Let's get something to eat," she said as she passed me on the way to the spread of food.

"You okay?" I asked.

"Yeah. Why wouldn't I be?"

"Um, because Caleb just got hijacked by the A-list crowd."

The A-listers were the top tier at Tundra School, the circle that included people like Jesse Kerr, Patrice Murray, Drew Chernov, and their many sycophants.

Lindsay snagged a dill-pickle spear from a bowl on the table and stared at Caleb across the crowd, a calculating look on her face. "Maybe we need to crash the popular crowd this year."

I crossed my arms and stared. "Seriously, did you smoke some crack this morning?"

"Hey, stranger things have happened." She used her pickle to point to someplace beyond my left shoulder. "Take that, for instance. Looks like all is not well in Most Popular Couple Land."

I slid into the food line behind Lindsay, just in time to see Patrice Murray angrily stalk away from Jesse in a pair of cute red wedges I was pretty sure they didn't even sell in Alaska. For one crazy, unexpected moment, I thought he deserved someone better than her. Somehow, Patrice had always managed to keep the adults snowed, but I'd seen more than one occasion of sheer bitchiness from her. Sure, Jesse wasn't my BFF or anything, but he seemed to be a halfway decent guy, and I have a particular dislike for spoiled, vindictive girls.

I squeezed ketchup onto the most charred-looking hot dog I could find, savoring the drama until I considered it could be because of me. If it were, Patrice was a bigger idiot than I'd thought. Like she had an iota to worry about from me. I had Spencer. Jesse Kerr wasn't even on my radar screen beyond his label as "neighbor."

Monica Belanov edged up to the table next to us. "Did you hear Jesse and Patrice going at it?" the petite point guard on the basketball team asked.

"Just saw, didn't hear," Lindsay said as she added wavy chips to her paper plate. "Noticed she left in a huff."

"Yeah, I don't know what started it, but I think they're kaput." Monica looked over her shoulder. "The line is already forming to be Jesse's next girlfriend. Any single guys better watch out, too, I guess." She rolled her eyes, continuing. "Sounded like Patrice plans to be boyfriendless for about three seconds."

"Bet whoever she sticks her claws into won't even have to be single," Lindsay said.

The heinous image of Patrice with Spencer burned a hole in the back of my eyeballs, and I choked on a chip.

Monica met my gaze. "You okay?"

I nodded.

"You better get on the ball and snatch up Spencer," Monica said. "He's got that whole hottie-nerd thing going on."

My stomach turned. The idea that Patrice might set her laser sights on Spencer made the realization that my feelings for him were common knowledge pale by comparison.

"As of last night, Spencer Isaacs is officially off the market," Lindsay said.

Monica's eyes widened as she looked at me again. "You go, girl. About damn time." She grabbed a brownie from a plate at the end of the table. "Though I personally don't think it'd hurt if Patrice tripped, say in the hall at school. I can't say I'd mind if she broke her nose, necessitating a humongous bandage."

I snorted at this. And apparently in doing so I tempted karma, because when I turned to head to the drink table, I tripped over someone's foot.

Instinctively, I reached out to catch myself, which only made things worse. I slammed into that same someone's chest. The owner of the chest caught me, and I looked up to find none other than Jesse Kerr, who was now wearing the contents of a beer can he shouldn't have had.

And he did *not* look happy.

Third-grade PE was going to kill me. Not only was I not athletic, but I constantly worried that I'd look like a fool in front of Spencer—especially today, when I was on his baseball team. I tried to put it out of my mind as I swung at the ball. Miraculously, I got a hit and made it to first base.

After two more batters sent me around the bases to home, I came face-to-face with Spencer. "Well?" I asked.

He gave me a teasing half smile. "You're okay, for a girl."

CHAPTER

Jesse righted me and glanced down at the liquid soaking his light-blue shirt.

This was exactly why I wasn't queen of the social scene. Before I could form an apology, he muttered a "sorry" of his own and hurried away toward the house.

"Way to go," Lindsay said. "We might have to rethink *you* cracking the A-list."

I stuck out my tongue, but she just smiled even wider.

Lindsay and Monica dived back into their conversation about the Snow Ball.

"Mom said if I wanted, she'd take me to Anchorage to get a dress for the ball," Monica said.

"Sweet," Lindsay replied. "You should totally ask Ryan Davis. I heard he's a good kisser."

Monica blushed as she caught sight of Ryan standing next to the grill, talking to Tyler Cookeson, center for the basketball team.

"You should go with Tyler," Monica said. "You two would look awesome together."

"Linds has set her sights elsewhere." I nodded toward the knot of populars surrounding Caleb.

"Oh, nice taste!" Monica gave Linds a high five.

I pushed aside my worries about Lindsay's fascination with Caleb and the inadvertent encounter with Jesse and let my friends' infectious excitement latch onto me.

"So, I guess you and Spencer are going if you're together," Monica said.

"Yeah."

"That's how they got together," Lindsay said. "Winter screwed up her courage and asked him."

"Nice. We've got to take things into our own hands. Can't depend on guys to make the first move. If we did, we'd be standing here when the next ice age started."

"Precisely," Lindsay said.

"Well, aren't we the three paragons of female empowerment," I said, drawing laughter from Linds and Monica.

As they started discussing how they were going to approach Caleb and Ryan, I pictured Spencer, gorgeous in a dark suit, escorting me, dancing with me and me alone. This year, the Snow Ball wouldn't be just another school function I skipped.

How was I supposed to wait three whole months? I could already see the school gym transformed into a glittering winter wonderland, something straight out of old Hollywood, a fantasy into which Spencer would guide me like Fred Astaire dancing with Ginger Rogers. My fingers itched to wrap around my drawing pencil, to design the ultimate dress. Something flowy and shimmery, a vibrant red that would contrast against the white decorations and the piles of snow that would no doubt cover Tundra in a thick, frozen blanket by then.

I lost myself in the daydream, in my thoughts of Spencer's arms around me, his warmth seeping into me, his eyes telling me he had waited his whole life to hold me close.

"What do you think?" Monica asked.

It took me a moment to realize she was addressing me, and I had no idea what she was asking about.

"Never mind," Lindsay said. "She's off in Lusting for Spencer Land now."

"Jeez, Linds. Could you say that a little louder? I'm not sure the oil-field workers at Prudhoe Bay heard you."

"You daydream during important conversations," Linds said in a fake Russian accent, "you pays the price."

To keep from laughing, I looked away from her. I noticed Mr. Kerr whispering something to Dad at the edge of the yard. A tight expression crossed Dad's face as he followed Mr. Kerr inside. Maybe there was some type of medical emergency. Whatever it was, I felt confident my dad would handle it. Nothing could ruin my high.

I thought of beer-soaked Jesse inside. If his dad caught him, my solid B-list status might slip even further.

Maybe I should go say something. But what could I do that wouldn't just make things worse? Lie and say that I bumped Jesse into someone older who had a beer? Maybe he'd already changed and gotten rid of the evidence anyway.

Why was I worrying about it? If the situation were

reversed, I doubted he'd do the same for me. I took a bite of chewy brownie.

"What is it?" Lindsay asked.

I didn't look at her, because I'd noticed Dad stepping out of the back door of the Kerrs' house, his face even tighter than before. "Something's going on," I said around my mouthful of chocolate. "Back in a minute."

I weaved my way through the crowd toward where Dad was talking to Mom. When I saw her hand go up to her mouth in shock, I quickened my steps.

"I'll let you know any news as soon as I can," Dad said, then kissed Mom on the cheek.

"What's going on?" I asked.

My parents jumped as if burned. My heart instinctively skipped.

Mom stepped forward. "We don't know the details yet. Everything may be fine."

The brownie lodged in my throat. "What are you talking about?"

Mom and Dad glanced at each other, a pained look passing between them. Some part of my brain registered the tears forming in Mom's eyes.

"I'm heading up to Katmai," Dad said. "A . . . a plane has gone down."

My vision tunneled, and my hearing grew muffled. My knees threatened to buckle. I glanced toward the mountains, noticed that the visibility conditions were worse up there now than when we'd arrived.

I shook my head. It couldn't be Spencer. It just couldn't be.

Mom reached for me, but I backed away. "No!" I scanned the crowd, frantic to confirm that Spencer had arrived and was safe, desperate to recapture the carefree, wondrous happiness of the previous minute. But his familiar face didn't appear among the others. "No, no, no."

I turned and ran, barely aware of anyone around me. I didn't know where I was going until I reached the end of our street and headed for Bristol Road. The airport. Spencer and Samuel, his instructor, would be there. Of that I was sure. And even if they weren't, Charlie Stevens, who ran the airport, would tell me everything was okay, that whoever had crashed was someone else. Not Spencer. Samuel was too experienced, Spencer too smart.

By the time I reached the airport, my breath was coming in ragged spurts. When my feet hit the linoleum floor in the lobby of the small, prefab building, they nearly slid out from under me. As I righted myself, I realized Charlie wasn't alone.

I edged closer to his office so I could hear what he was saying.

"I'm so sorry," I heard Charlie say softly.

The sound of Spencer's mother's cry froze my heart solid. The pain of realization pierced me from every direction. I stood, unable to move, unable to breathe.

God, I prayed, please let me have misunderstood. Let this be an awful, terrible, cruel dream.

But the sobs from inside Charlie's office were too real, too raw.

With a guttural, wounded cry of my own, I crumpled to the floor.

I gritted my teeth as Patrice Murray sold two more boxes of Campfire Girl candy. I still couldn't believe she'd stolen my spot outside the door to Tundra Foods, that she was down to a single box. I couldn't believe I had to put up with her for seven more years. I looked down at my ten remaining boxes, then at the waning light. Patrice was going to win the digital camera given to the girl who sold all of her candy first.

I looked up when I heard someone approach my table. "Oh, hey, Spencer."

"I need something sweet."

I reached for a box to hand to him.

"I'll take all ten boxes," he said.

CHAPTER

The hours crept by with an agonizing slowness. They were hours in which we heard nothing from my dad. The phone rang several times, but it was never the one call I craved.

Lindsay sat beside me, holding my hand. "I'm sure he's fine," she said. "I bet your dad is with him now."

I nodded—I wanted desperately to believe in the determined truth of her words, though they were laced with doubt. "I wish they'd call."

"You know there's no reception in huge parts of the park. The bears don't have much use for cell phones." She tried to smile.

I knew she wanted to lighten the mood, like always. Like when her mom and dad fought. Like the time in seventh grade when I'd become convinced that Spencer liked Tia Vanderhugh.

As night began to fall, Mom tried to send Lindsay home, but she wouldn't budge. Spencer was one of her best friends, too. I ignored the fact that she grew quieter with each passing minute.

The phone continued to ring, but still nothing. I felt so

exhausted that it became difficult to move, and I laid my head in Lindsay's lap. She ran her fingers absently through my long hair. I closed my eyes and focused on my mental image of Spencer bunking down in the woods for the night, keeping warm until help arrived. He was strong, resourceful. I had nothing to worry about. I mouthed the words a few times. "I have nothing to worry about."

Mom cooked dinner, but despite my determined confidence in Spencer's safety, I had no appetite. I'd eat when I saw Spencer again, I told myself. I was only vaguely aware of Mom and Lindsay sitting at the kitchen table with their plates of spaghetti. The normalcy of this small gesture was comforting.

We watched TV throughout the evening, but nothing much penetrated my thoughts. It was just something to stare at, a series of flickering lights and movement. The only thing that made it through the thick barrier around me was the sound of the clock ticking on the wall. It drove me crazy, so much so that if Mom hadn't been in the room, I would have shattered it with my shoe.

Lindsay sat in the recliner, and I nearly gave in to tears when I saw the worry darkening her lovely features.

Lindsay couldn't doubt, she just couldn't.

My brain began to reengage when the ten o'clock news came on.

I lifted myself to a sitting position. "Turn it up."

Mom hesitated before complying.

"Investigators are still determining the cause of a plane crash in Katmai National Park earlier today, but witnesses on the ground tell KTUU that the Piper Super Cub seemed to stall before slamming into the side of Dumpling Mountain."

The video cut to shots from a helicopter above the crash site. Thick fog covered the area. I scooted forward, straining to see any glimpse of Spencer.

When the image on the screen finally changed, cutting through the fog and revealing what looked like a red wing bent at an impossible angle, Lindsay uttered a strangled sob. I ignored her, focusing on the screen, desperate for an image of hope.

The anchor's sudden reappearance on the TV startled me.

"The names of the two individuals on board are being withheld until family members can be contacted, but we can confirm that the plane took off from the airstrip in Tundra, near Bristol Bay."

Mom clicked off the TV as the anchors moved to another story.

"Oh my God," Lindsay said.

"Don't!" My voice was harsh. Lindsay looked wounded when our eyes met, but I didn't apologize. I couldn't let anyone near me doubt. How would Spencer feel if he thought we had so little faith in him?

I shifted closer to Mom, unwilling to let negative thoughts bury themselves in my mind. I was holding on by the thinnest of threads and I feared talking would snap it.

More minutes ticked by. I noticed Lindsay had curled up and fallen asleep, her face worried even at rest.

I let my eyes wander around the living room, taking in

images so familiar I didn't even think about them anymore. Photos of me at different ages, a bookshelf full of books about every aspect of Alaska, the shelf of carved moose belonging to my dad, another of native-carved ivory—miniature animals carved by Lester Konekuk. Mom added a new piece each fall when we descended on the fall craft fair.

Despite my best efforts to stay awake, to keep the vigil, I felt myself getting drowsy. Sleep held more than its normal appeal. Perhaps there I could cease to worry and stop having horrible images pop into my head, even though I was determined to stay positive.

Finally, Mom pulled the afghan off the back of the couch and spread it over me. "Get some rest, sweetie."

I wanted to argue but couldn't find the energy.

I awoke sometime later when I heard the door close. I fought the post-sleep grogginess and sat up as I noticed my dad coming in the side door. I opened my mouth to ask about Spencer, but I froze when Dad turned toward us and I saw the expression on his face: tired, drawn, devastated.

A cry clawed its way out of my throat as the truth hit me. Spencer was gone.

I don't know how long I cried, or when I drifted off again, but when I woke sometime later, my head was pounding, my eyes puffy and aching. I felt as if I'd been dropped from the top of a tree.

Lindsay lay under a blanket in the recliner, asleep and curled into a tight ball. I knew the look by then. It was how she slept when she was upset.

I could hear voices from somewhere in the house. When I had pulled myself upright and waited for my head to stop spinning, I realized they were coming from the dining room on the other side of the kitchen, two rooms away. My parents were using hushed tones, clearly meant to keep me from hearing. I heard other voices join theirs. I moved carefully, eager to avoid detection.

Some part of my brain screamed at me to turn around and go back to the couch—that I didn't want to hear whatever they were saying. But some other masochistic part of me trudged forward.

I stopped right outside the room, resting in the shadows of the darkened kitchen. Mom and Dad sat at the end of the dining room table, Mom's hands wrapped around Dad's. He slumped like someone totally defeated, as if he'd aged twenty years since this morning. Mom lifted one of her hands to wipe tears from her face. I choked up at the sight.

The Kerrs sat across from them—their faces sad, too. Movement in the corner of the room caught my attention, and my eyes met Jesse's. He started to open his mouth, but I shook my head. I could tell he didn't think my presence was a good idea, but that wasn't for him to decide.

"As soon as I saw the wreck, all I could think was, 'How am I going to tell Winter?'" Dad's voice broke.

I almost revealed myself then. I couldn't remember the last time I'd seen Dad cry; maybe not since his father had died seven years ago. As a doctor, he dealt with death all the time. Eventually, he'd acquired the professional detachment all doctors had to have in order to survive their jobs. But not tonight.

"I still can't believe it," Mom said. "I keep thinking I'll wake up, and this will have all been a horrible dream."

"I wish it were. God, how I wish that." He swallowed hard.

"Can you tell what happened?" Mr. Kerr asked. "They said on the news the plane might have stalled."

Dad shook his head. "We don't know. It's possible the fog caused them to get too close to the mountain, then they tried to climb too quickly and lost their lift. The NTSB is up there now, but I don't know how they could possibly figure it out." He ran his hand back over his hair in a gesture I didn't see from him often. He glanced at Jesse, pausing before deciding to continue. "We didn't even find the bodies. We couldn't tell if the fire consumed them or if the bears had beaten us there."

My hands slid away from where I'd been gripping the edge of the doorway. I stumbled as I turned, drawing everyone's attention. I saw them move toward me in slow motion, Jesse the quickest. I barely heard Mom say my name before the world went black.

"I wish I could draw like that," Spencer said as he looked at my drawing of our art teacher, Mrs. Spiro.

I liked how his compliment made me feel warm inside. I liked how he smiled at me.

CHAPTER

Sunlight slanting into my room woke me. I wanted to scream. This brightness wasn't right when I felt so lost, so dark.

Somehow I'd gotten to my room. I realized I must have fainted, and that my dad had probably carried me to bed. I burrowed back under the covers and wished away the bright, shiny world outside. I cursed the sun, the expanse of blue sky, the clear air around the distant mountains. Why hadn't they appeared for Spencer's flight? Why only when it was too late to do any good?

A fresh sob tumbled out of me, and I pressed my thick comforter against my eyes. I thought I was cried out, until I felt the bed dip behind me and realized it was Lindsay. She wrapped herself around me, and the two of us sobbed together.

"I can't believe he's gone," she whispered into my hair.

I couldn't find any words to respond. Nothing of me remained but tears and slashing pain. My only escape was the occasional descent into sleep.

About mid-afternoon, I woke to find Lindsay no longer

beside me. Still, I didn't get out of bed. Instead, I reached out and nearly fumbled my cell phone off my nightstand onto the floor. I pulled it to me and flipped it open. I scrolled through the photos of Spencer behind the counter at Tundra Books, fishing pole in hand at the river, goofing off by flexing his biceps after making a home run in PE class.

I ran my thumb across the screen and wished I could touch him for real, feel his arms around me again. Taste his kiss.

I only stirred from the bed to go to the bathroom. Each time I returned, exhaustion claimed me. I kept thinking that maybe one of the times I'd just not wake up. Part of me hoped it would happen.

Eventually, I couldn't sleep or cry anymore. I stared at the waning daylight with dry, puffy eyes and a hollow soul. How was it possible that Spencer had been gone for only a day? It felt like so much longer.

The door to my bedroom creaked open, and I recognized the sound of Mom's steps as she approached my bed. She sat behind me and rubbed her hand gently over my messy, unwashed hair.

"Winter, I've got dinner ready."

"I'm not hungry." My voice sounded raw, like fate had sandpapered my vocal cords.

"I know, honey. But you need to eat. You'll make yourself sick."

"I don't care." How could I eat when all I wanted was to die?

I heard her intake of breath. "Oh, don't say that," she said in a gentle, soothing tone.

As fat, hot, salty drops spilled over yet again, anger bloomed violently within me. "It's not fair!" I screamed. "I love him."

Mom turned me into her arms and rocked back and forth with me the way she had when I was little. She didn't try to hide her own heartache.

"Why, Mom? Why?"

"I don't know." She kissed the top of my head. I heard in her pain that she couldn't make this hurt go away for me.

After that, Mom didn't push me to come downstairs or eat. She did, however, bring up a bowl of potato soup (my favorite) and fresh-baked bread. She left the tray on my desk, where it remained untouched.

The moon shone bright and huge in the sky. I'd slept so much during the day that my body now refused me that escape. I let my eyes roam my room, covered with movie posters. *Pride and Prejudice*, *300*, *Titanic*, *X-Men*, *Lord of the Rings*. Basically any movie in which the story and the costumes made a winning combination.

But while they'd often given me inspiration for my own costume designs, now they hung there: lifeless, reminders of a me that that no longer existed.

I slid my aching body out of bed and onto the floor in front of my bookshelves. I ran my fingertips over the spines of the many titles I'd bought at Tundra Books, the bookstore owned by Spencer's parents. I'd memorized long ago what Spencer had written inside each book.

I caressed the title along the edge of *Prince Caspian*. I closed my eyes, could see Spencer's handwriting inside.

"Wish you, Lindsay, and I could travel to Narnia."

My fingers traveled to the next several books, the complete *Anne of Green Gables* collection Spencer had gotten me for my twelfth birthday. I opened the first, to one of the blank pages at the beginning. My heart ached as I looked at the quote from the book I'd read over and over again until it was burned into my memory.

"I think you may be a kindred spirit after all. Happy birthday. Love, Spencer."

It was the first time the word *love* had traveled between us.

Next, I pulled a photo album from the end of the shelf. I didn't think my heart could ache any more, but seeing all the happy photos of Spencer made me feel as if the world had ended.

For Spencer, it had. No more smiles. No more happy photos. No more telling me—or anyone else—that he loved me.

God, how could a life like Spencer's just . . . *end*?

When I woke late in the morning, I was still on the floor, one arm cradling the album. Someone had draped a blanket over me: Lindsay, at least according to the note she'd left next to two strawberry pastries.

"I stopped by this morning, but I didn't want to wake you. See you after school. Luv you."

School? She was going to school? I read the words again, but they still made no sense.

Lindsay's familiar handwriting stared up at me, and I hated myself for wishing she'd stay away. I'd thought she was hurting, too, but if she were, how could she go back? Going back was inconceivable to me. I didn't want to see or talk to anyone. All I wanted was to cocoon myself in this room and never emerge.

My stomach growled at the sight of the pastries. Even though they were no longer piping hot, I found myself reaching for one. Apparently, my body's instinct to survive wouldn't be denied.

My cell phone rang, and I grabbed it, desperately hoping to see Spencer's name.

But it was the school's number. It had to be Lindsay, who didn't have a cell of her own. I turned the phone off when the beep told me she'd left a message, then I pitched it at the thick red carpet.

I spent the day curled in my overstuffed red chair in the corner next to the window, my feet propped on the matching ottoman. I looked through my photo albums at least a dozen times.

I couldn't remember the last time I'd been in my room this long without popping in a DVD, but those fictional stories no longer held any allure, not even any chance at escape.

Mom came in with a chicken-salad sandwich and chips around lunchtime. She must have thought I was asleep, because she slid the plate onto my desk and walked quietly back toward the door.

"You didn't go to work," I accused.

"No. I wanted to be here for you."

I should have told her I was fine, but I couldn't. It was too big of a lie.

Neither of us seemed to know what to say next, so she offered me a weak smile and walked back out.

But what was there to say? Sorry the boy you've loved since you were eight finally kissed you, then died the next day?

She couldn't even say that, because she didn't know about our kisses. The only person who did was Lindsay, and for some reason, now I wished she didn't.

I curled farther down into the chair and refocused my meandering thoughts, visualizing Spencer alive and working his way down the mountain toward me. I daydreamed of all the things we'd do together. Our first date. The Snow Ball. Admitting we loved each other. Eventually expressing our love for each other, maybe beneath a thick blanket while the northern lights performed their magical dance overhead.

I liked these fantasies.

Reality intruded in the form of Lindsay. How had I not heard the front door?

"Hey." She sat on the ottoman at my feet and eyed me with her worried expression. "Have you eaten today?"

I pointed toward the half-eaten sandwich.

"Lots of people at school asked about you."

Several ticks of the clock went by. "I just . . . couldn't."

She stood and walked to the window, staring out at the waning day. "I couldn't sit at home."

I still didn't know how she could face going to school so soon after our best friend had died, but I didn't have the energy to figure it out. Or to examine the anger that was welling up inside me.

I lowered my gaze to the open photo album on my lap, at a picture of Spencer and me at last year's Labor Day cookout. I closed my eyes and remembered the details of the day.

"Here you go," Spencer had said as he extended a plate piled with food to me.

"Dude, that's enough food for three people," I'd replied as I looked at the huge barbecue sandwich, mountain of chips, and two brownies.

"You need to eat. Helps you heal."

I rolled my eyes at him. "I twisted my ankle, genius. I don't have the flu."

He shrugged, sat on the ground beside my lawn chair, and dug into his own food. "I feel guilty, so I'm groveling, okay?"

"Oh, yes, this is your fault, isn't it?" I pointed at my wrapped ankle propped on another lawn chair. I'd tripped while chasing him up the stairs after he'd come into the living room, wearing the flapper-style costume I'd been working on for Halloween.

"Yep. Guess you'll have to think of an appropriate way to scold me," he said suggestively, prompting me to give him a smack to the back of his head.

I wanted to laugh at the memory, but I couldn't. I ran my fingertips over his glossy, smiling image. I'd been an idiot not to tell him how I felt sooner.

Only the impending start of our senior year, the last year we might spend together, had prompted me to risk our friendship by telling him I liked him much more than just as a friend. I could still feel the soft, warm, tentative first kiss we'd shared on the banks of the Naknek River and how it had ignited the boom, color, and sizzle of the Fourth of July inside me. The taste of the cherry Twizzlers he constantly munched on at the store still lingered.

Lindsay took my hand and squeezed it. I opened my eyes, hating her for pulling me out of my sweet memories. I pulled my hand out of hers and stared out the window. Another day fading away. Another day without Spencer.

I didn't even turn my head when Lindsay sighed and slid off the ottoman. A few seconds passed before she returned and took my hand again. She'd been running a bath.

"Come on."

I followed wordlessly, thankful she'd skipped the platitudes. When she left me alone, I sank onto the closed toilet seat and stared at the steamy, foam-filled water, inhaling the lavender scent of the bath salts. I silently scolded myself—it seemed wrong to indulge in comfort when Spencer might never enjoy warmth and smell favorite scents again.

As if my body had a will of its own, I found myself slipping into the water. When the delicious warmth soaked into me, my chin began to quiver.

"Forgive me," I whispered.

"Which one should I wear to the academic competition in Anchorage?" Spencer asked as he held up two shirts, one striped in various shades of blue and one sporting a hideous orange-and-purple check pattern.

"Hello, you're twelve. Can't you dress yourself?" I asked.

"Without your expert opinion. That would just be silly," he said dramatically.

"The blue one," I said, though I thought Spencer would look good in anything.

CHAPTER

5

On Friday, three days after the crash, Mom came to my room early. Dressed for work, she sat on the edge of my rumpled bed and took my hand. "I don't feel right leaving you here. Maybe you could come with me. It might help to be with your friends."

"Was that what Lindsay said?" I knew it was irrational, but the hurt and anger I felt seeped out anyway.

"Winter." Her tone scolded but not strongly. "Everyone handles grief in different ways."

I retrieved my hand and rolled over, turning my back to her. Part of me knew she was right, but I felt like my emotions were coming apart at the seams, flying in random directions. The anger seemed to keep some of the pain at bay. At least sometimes I convinced myself of that for a few minutes.

Mom sighed. "Call me if you need anything, then. Or even if you just want me to come home."

"I just want to be alone." This was a lie. I wanted Spencer there with me—kissing me, holding me.

I listened as Mom left the room. When I heard her voice outside, I dragged myself to the window. She stood in the driveway talking to Jesse Kerr, but I couldn't make out their words. I saw him shake his head, and she got into her car and backed out of the gravel drive onto the street.

Jesse didn't follow her. Instead, he looked up at my window. I gasped when his eyes met mine. The startling thought that he might try to come up and see me—offer me some empty comfort—made me step back from the window, out of view.

I sank onto my ottoman and dropped my head into my upturned hands. If a simple glance could unnerve me so much, no wonder my mom seemed concerned. I wondered if I looked as brittle as I felt.

The walls of my bedroom began to close in on me. I wanted to take the fake Oscar, which Spencer and Lindsay had gotten me two birthdays ago, and use it to bust every breakable object in my room. My movie posters no longer held wonder and dreams, and if I'd had more strength, I would have ripped them down and torn them to shreds. Dreams were now a thing of the past for me. And for Spencer.

I knew I couldn't concentrate long enough to lose myself in reading or homework. My DVD collection could melt, for all I cared. When I looked at my sketch pad, I had to fight the urge to set fire to it. Part of me wished the walls would literally close in and squash me like a trash compactor. But that part of myself that forced me to eat—and had driven me to sink myself into the bathwater—wanted to escape this madness caused by my isolation.

So I emerged from my room like a prisoner thrust upon a world I no longer remembered how to live in. Like Morgan Freeman's character in *The Shawshank Redemption*.

Dad was already gone, off tending to the infected and broken citizens of Tundra. I meandered into the kitchen and pulled a sleeve of Ritz crackers from the cupboard. I trudged from the kitchen to the living room, surveying the room like I hadn't seen it in years. Suddenly feeling as if I couldn't breathe indoor air another moment, I wandered onto the deck out back that faced the thinly wooded area at the back of our property.

I closed my eyes. Sounds and scents became sharper. The breeze carried the scent of firs and the faintest hint of the coming winter. Beyond the stirring of the air through the trees and the belch of Lane Berkley's old pickup down the street, I heard boat motors on the river and the barely discernible lap of waves against the riverbanks.

Despite my fatigue, I headed for the river. It took me three times as long to reach it as normal. I wasn't sure if it was because of my exhaustion or because I was afraid how I'd react to the spot where the relationship between Spencer and I had changed.

As I neared the riverbank, I didn't cry. Instead, the memory of our first kiss made me smile.

The call of arctic terns overhead caused me to look up. I watched as their dark red beaks disappeared to the south.

I was so immersed in the sensory details around me that I jumped when I heard someone's footsteps crunch on the gravel path. I expected one of my parents or Lindsay—*not* Jesse Kerr. The likelihood of him standing there, staring, was so unthinkable that I wondered if I'd begun to hallucinate.

"What are you doing here?"

"Just wanted to make sure you were okay."

"I'm not going to jump in the river—if that's what you're worried about."

"I'm glad to hear that. I was concerned."

I jerked my gaze to him. Jesse's expression really did look like concern. My world tilted a bit more on its axis.

He shifted his weight from one foot to the other and glanced down for a moment before meeting my eyes again. "I'm really sorry about Spencer. I know how you must be feeling."

His words sent a surge of blazing anger through me. "You could never know how I feel," I spit at him. How could someone like him, whose life didn't seem to have any bumps beyond a fight with his girlfriend, possibly understand?

Jesse looked startled. He pressed his lips together as if to prevent himself from speaking. His eyes were troubled. For a moment, I felt bad that I'd snapped. It wasn't his fault. I must seem like Jekyll and Hyde to him.

But hearing him speak Spencer's name nearly made me cry, even though I knew I should be totally empty by now. I redirected my gaze toward the river, unwilling to show my vulnerability in front of Jesse. We stood like that for a few moments.

"Shouldn't you be at school?" I asked, wishing he'd go away.

"School can wait."

I looked away. It made no sense that Jesse was skipping school while Lindsay was there, walking those halls that were empty of Spencer. I stared out across the river to the tundra beyond, but Jesse didn't make any move to leave.

When I glanced at him, he'd turned his gaze toward the opposite side of the river, too. Something passed across his features, but I couldn't discern what.

"It's not hard to figure out why you're hurting. Spencer's death hit you hard. That much was clear when you passed out the other night. You didn't even wake up when you were carried upstairs."

"Did my dad tell you that?"

"No."

I let his words soak in for several seconds. Did he mean? . . . "You? You're the one who carried me upstairs?"

He'd been in my room? No guy had ever been in my room except Spencer. It was wrong to think of Jesse there, seeing my things—privy to more of who I was than almost anyone, Spencer and Lindsay excluded.

Jesse met my eyes with his dark ones. "Yes. Your dad was exhausted, and my dad has a bad back."

I looked away, unable to face him any longer. "I . . . I'm . . ."

"No need to be embarrassed."

I wasn't embarrassed. Okay, so I was, but that wasn't all of what I was feeling. The whole idea of Jesse lifting me in his arms and carrying me up the stairs to my room felt . . . odd, like something out of some other girl's dreams. If I had ever dreamed such a scenario, I would have cast Spencer in the role, not Jesse. But Jesse hadn't had to be at my house that night, especially after we'd run into each other at the cookout. But he had been, and he'd been decent enough to help when I'd needed it.

I turned to say something—maybe an unexpected thank you—but I'd waited too long. He was already walking away.

I couldn't begin to explain why his departure left me feeling confused. And with an odd sense of longing.

Spencer looked out across the gym floor at our seventh-grade classmates at our first school dance. He shrugged and glanced over at me.

"Guess we might as well dance," he said. "Since we're here and all."

CHAPTER

6

Walking into Spencer's memorial service on Saturday felt like an out-of-body experience. Nothing seemed real—not Reverend Blake's words as he greeted us at the door, not the many fragrant flower arrangements perfuming the air, not Lesa and Kristen, who had flown home from college to be with me and to say their own good-byes. They'd known Spencer all his life, had treated him like the little brother they didn't have.

All the voices around me sounded muffled and very far away. I imagined that must be what it felt like to be high—disconnected from everything and everyone around me.

I spotted Monica Belanov hugging Lindsay near a large photo of a smiling Spencer. I remembered that picture. It'd been during Tundra Books' midnight release party for *Harry Potter and the Deathly Hallows*. Somehow, the choice of that photo rang perfect, and also tremendously wrong.

"Come on, sweetie," Lesa said, as she guided me forward.

I wanted to run away and pretend this wasn't happening, this finality to Spencer's life. But I didn't have the strength.

I'd probably trip in the black Nine West pumps I was wearing and fall face-first in the church vestibule.

My sisters must have sensed my hesitation as we headed for the front of the sanctuary, because they held on to me even more firmly as we walked.

When we reached Monica and Lindsay, Monica hugged me. I held on to her with what little strength I had. Lindsay had difficulty meeting my eyes, but after a moment's hesitation, she pulled me to her. We clung to each other until Mom steered us toward Spencer's parents.

I balked. "I can't. I'm not ready."

Mom tried to guide me forward, but I refused to move.

"Just give me a couple minutes." I spun around and headed toward the restroom as if it were my salvation.

When I reached the rose and off-white sitting area for the restroom, I braced myself against the sink and tried to get my ragged breathing under control. I was concentrating on an exhale when Lindsay came through the door. Without a word, she wetted a paper towel and handed it to me. I pressed it against my forehead. In the mirror, I noticed the dark circles under her eyes: the red-rimmed evidence of earlier tears.

I shook my head slowly. "I can't go back out there. I can't face this."

Lindsay's look hardened as she met my eyes in the mirror. "You can, and you will. I know you're hurting, but today isn't about you. We have to be strong for Spencer's parents. They've lost their only child." Lindsay's voice broke, but she cleared her throat in an attempt at hiding it.

Her words sank through my sorrow. Some tiny reserve of strength told me I could be brave for the next hour or two, for Spencer's parents, who were like a second mom and dad to me.

My head spun as I walked slowly toward the door.

When I reentered the sanctuary and approached Mr. and Mrs. Isaacs, I saw the distraught look on Spencer's mom's face. In that moment, I hated Lindsay for making me do this.

Mrs. Isaacs wrapped me in her arms and squeezed me like it might bring Spencer back. "He loved you so much," she said in my ear.

I ached that I'd never hear him say those words to me the way I'd wanted. I swallowed past the painful lump in my throat. "I loved him, too," I whispered.

I sat through the service, listening to eulogies for the boy I'd loved with all my heart. I stared at his picture, half believing it would spring to life.

"Winter Craig has asked to say a few words," Reverend Blake said.

I still couldn't believe I'd offered to speak. But as I'd looked at my bookshelves the night before and realized that books written by Spencer would never be among them, I'd felt compelled to share some of his words.

My entire body shook as I rose to my feet. Through some miracle, I made it to the podium without collapsing. I looked out at all the faces I'd known my entire life and choked back a sob. I opened the paper I held and smoothed it atop the podium.

"Spencer wanted to do two things in life—fly and write. He wanted to fly around the world and write about what he saw from the air." I swallowed past the giant lump in my throat and gripped the sides of the podium more tightly. "'The Ribbon,' by Spencer Isaacs." I cleared my throat and began to read.

"'The river, silver and shining, undulates like a ribbon in the breeze. It breathes its foggy breath and winks at me as the sun kisses its surface. It caresses the fish below its glassy surface and tempts the birds of every stripe to taste of it.'"

By the time I finished the passage, I knew everyone in the room would never look at the Naknek the same way again. Spencer had taken something we all saw every day and made it magical—the way he was for me.

It took me a moment to unclasp my fingers from where they'd been holding me upright and for my brain to tell my legs to move. By the time I reached my seat, I was utterly exhausted.

The sound of someone else's tears made me glance around the room. Beyond Spencer's Aunt Barbara, I spotted Jesse. He was watching me. I quickly returned my attention to the front of the sanctuary, where the choir began singing "Come to Jesus."

I bit my quivering lip as the lyrics assaulted me. Lindsay gripped my left hand, and I blinked back the tears that wanted so desperately to break free. I stared at the flowers and photo, and my anguish finally spilled down my cheeks, along my neck, and into the top of my black dress.

When the choir sang, "And with your final heartbeat,

kiss the world good-bye," I squeezed Lindsay's hand even harder. I felt her shaking with restrained sorrow.

God, help me through this.

The smell of fried chicken assaulted me as we approached the potluck spread provided by the ladies of the church, and I had to swallow hard to keep from being sick.

"He was such a good boy," I heard the minister's mother say to Mr. Henning, the school principal.

The potluck proved to be too much. I had to get out of the building, away from all these sad people, before I suffocated. I mumbled that I was going to get a slice of pie and headed for the far tables laden with desserts. Why was there so much food? How could people eat at a time like this?

I walked past the desserts, into the hall, and through the back door.

I started to fall apart well before I got home. By the time I rushed through the front door of our normally comforting log house, I was ripping at the buttons of my dress. I couldn't get it off fast enough. It felt like it was sucking the life out of me, hiding it in the midnight weave of the fabric.

I tossed the dress on my bed and threw the black hose in the trash can. I screamed as I took one of the dark heels and threw it with as much force as I could at the wall, puncturing Keira Knightley's face on my *Pride and Prejudice* poster.

I pulled on a pair of sweatpants and an old Tundra School T-shirt and collapsed into my corner chair. I stared at the black funeral dress. Rage bubbled inside me until I leaped from the chair and grabbed the dress. I fumbled in the nightstand drawer, searching for the box of matches I used to light candles.

I nearly tripped down the stairs in my haste to get to the backyard, to make this damned dress go away forever. Several feet away from the house, I dropped to the ground and lit a match. Twice, matches sparked, then died before I could bring them to the dress's hem. The third only caused a bit of a stinking smolder.

"Damn it! Why won't you burn?" Tears streamed down my face.

"Winter."

I spun to see Jesse standing a few feet away.

"What are you doing?"

I surged to my feet. "Go away! You don't belong here. This isn't for you." I returned to striking and cursing the matches, tossing them aside when they refused to cooperate. "Burn, damn you, burn!"

Jesse touched my shoulder, and I launched myself at him. "Leave me alone!" I hit his shoulder with my fist. "Just leave me alone." My voice broke as I hit him again and again.

He used his strength to grab my hands and stop the assault. I continued to struggle until the last bit of fight died away. A horrible sob surged out of me. Jesse finally released my wrists and pulled me to him, pressing me against his chest. "Why did he leave me?" I whispered.

Jesse didn't answer. He just held me, keeping me from collapsing as the world's worst pain poured out of me.

"What's that?" I asked as I watched Spencer hanging a poster in Tundra Books.

"Mom wants these love quotes all over the store for Valentine's Day," he replied. He turned the quote so I could see it.

"There is only one happiness in life, to love and be loved.
—George Sand"

I turned my attention to the rack of paperbacks next to me so he wouldn't see how the words made my heart flutter.

CHAPTER

7

Things didn't get any easier after the memorial service. First, the horrible, embarrassing breakdown with Jesse. Now, I stood outside the door to the school on Monday morning, wondering how I'd ever make it through the first hour, let alone the entire day. The familiar concrete structure felt like a foreign land as I stared at it.

A hand at my back made me jump.

"I'm sorry, Winter," said Mrs. Schuler, the guidance counselor. "I didn't mean to startle you." She looked at me sympathetically. "I just wanted to let you know that if you need to talk today, or anytime, I'm here."

"Thank you," I mumbled, before hurrying away from her and into the school.

The last day I'd walked these halls, Spencer had been with me.

I ran my hands over the lightweight navy-blue sweater Spencer had bought me for Christmas last year. Its cuffs were long and lacy—he'd said it looked like something a costume designer would wear. I tried to draw some strength from it. I felt more alone, now that the gulf between Lindsay and me kept widening.

I hadn't realized until I'd been walking to school this morning that I hadn't talked to her since the scene in the bathroom at the church. Had we ever gone a day without at least a phone call?

Suddenly, I dreaded seeing her. I didn't know what to say, didn't want to talk to anyone. I ducked into the restroom. A group of girls standing next to the sinks stopped talking when they saw me. One gave me a sad smile. I tried to smile back, but it felt more like a grimace. I hurried into a stall, sinking onto the closed toilet. I tried desperately to calm down. Why had my parents made me come back so soon? Only a week had passed since the crash.

Dad had taken my hand this morning, holding it firmly in his own. "Be honest with yourself. You knew Spencer better than most people. Would he want this?"

I'd relaxed my hand in Dad's and let the awful realization sink in. I could actually hear Spencer telling me to get my pitiful butt out of bed.

As I walked back to my locker, I felt as if I were slogging through thick mud. Each step sapped a bit more of what little energy I had. I caught whispers as I passed by groups of my classmates.

"She looks so pale."

"I can't imagine how she must feel."

"Didn't Jesse Kerr follow her home from the memorial service?"

At this, I shot a look at Tazzie Blue. She sucked in a breath and lowered her eyes, embarrassed that I'd heard.

God, how was I going to face Jesse after what had happened? How could I have broken down like that? I scanned the hallway and didn't see him. I knew it was probably too much to hope for, but maybe I could avoid what was sure to be an uncomfortable confrontation.

By the time I reached my locker, I had to lean my head against the cool metal to catch my breath.

"Hey," Lindsay said next to me. "I wondered if you were coming today."

"Not much choice."

"Where did you go on Saturday?" Was that a hint of accusation in her voice, or was I imagining it?

"Home. I couldn't stay any longer. I felt like I was going to suffocate."

"I didn't want to be there, either."

"I know that," I snapped, realizing too late how mean I sounded. I didn't want to—I just didn't seem to be able to help myself. I closed my eyes for a moment and tried to calm down. "It's just been a horrible week," I said, as I looked at her again.

Lindsay opened her mouth to say something, but she quickly stopped herself. "I'll see you later," she said, slamming the door to her locker.

Instinct told me something else was on her mind, but I couldn't muster the energy to go after her and ask what. Why had she looked so tense?

I inhaled a deep breath to prepare myself before opening my locker. But it didn't soften the punch to my heart when

I saw all the photos taped inside: ones of Spencer alone, another of him with his arms around me when we were still just friends, others of the two of us with Lindsay. Tears pooled in my eyes, but I blinked them away. No way was I crying at school. On top of my grief, I could only take so much embarrassment. And I'd filled that quota on Saturday.

With one final look at the photos, I grabbed my books and closed the door.

"Hey, Winter," Monica said when I turned and saw her a few lockers down. "Are you okay?"

Hell, no, I wasn't okay. But I wasn't going to cry on the shoulder of everyone I met. I nodded and headed past her down the hall.

I stopped as I reached Spencer's locker and ran my hand down it. I imagined I could see his fingerprints all over it, that I could feel his touch.

How could I feel hollow and filled with despair at the same time?

Throughout the morning, I went through the motions of "normal." Friends hugged me in the hallways. Teachers extended my homework deadlines. I knew everyone meant well, but all the interactions felt awkward and distant. Like only my body came to school, while my heart was in the mountains looking for Spencer.

English class was the worst. I balked at the door and stared at the empty seat that yawned like a black hole next to my own. When some of my classmates began to edge around me to get into the room, I headed to my desk and tried to ignore Spencer's empty one. But it proved impossible.

Nervousness shot through me when Jesse entered the room. His tall, hockey player frame seemed to fill the room. I tried to act like I hadn't noticed him, but he stopped by my desk.

"Hey. How are you?"

I was drained, panicked, and dying to run away and hide.

"Fine," I said.

He lingered, and it made me want to scream. I didn't know where this hostility was coming from.

Only when Mrs. Miller entered the room did he walk down the row to his seat at the back of the class. I was so unnerved that I dropped my pencil. Hannah Stevens, who sat in the seat in front of Spencer's empty one, picked it up and gave it back to me with an understanding smile.

It struck me that *everyone* was being understanding but Lindsay. Irritation at that, on top of everything else, made it next to impossible to concentrate in any of my morning classes.

When the lunch period rolled around, I didn't have any appetite. I wandered into the cafeteria and straight to one of the tables by the windows. When someone slid into a chair opposite me, I expected Lindsay or maybe Monica. Not Jesse Kerr.

"Why are you sitting here?" He normally sat with the A-listers. Had he changed lunch tables since his breakup with Patrice?

He extended a cheeseburger toward me. "You don't have any lunch."

"I'm not hungry."

He returned the cheeseburger to his own plate, fiddled with the edge of the plastic tray. "Are you mad at me?"

Yes. But why? Because he'd seen me at my worst? Because I'd been goofing off with him while Spencer had crashed into a mountain? Because he was alive and Spencer wasn't?

I glanced at him, saw the confusion in his dark eyes. I dropped my gaze to the empty table in front of me. "No."

"Don't worry about what happened," he said. "I won't say anything."

I let his words sink in for a few seconds, surprised he'd picked up on my concern that people might get the wrong idea about us. A concern I hadn't realized until now. How would it look if people knew I'd let him be the one to hold me while I cried out my grief? I still couldn't believe it'd happened.

"Thank you." I hoped he understood the significance of my words. The whispers in the hallway were bad enough. Not to mention the fact he was sitting at my table with me, alone. I didn't dare look around the room to see if everyone was watching, gossiping.

We sat in silence while he ate. I stared out the window. Despite the current strain between Lindsay and me, I found myself wishing she would come in and save me from this awkwardness. I searched frantically for something to say, then remembered I still owed Jesse an apology.

"I'm sorry."

"About what? Saturday?"

I looked at him. "Well, yes."

"You don't have to apologize."

I lowered my eyes to my hands in my lap picking at my cuticles. "I also meant about the day of the cookout, when I ran into you."

He waved away my words. "No big deal. I just wasn't having the best day. But it's nothing now."

I suspected he meant in light of Spencer's death, but I wasn't ready to start talking about that. First, I had to try to make it through one day without falling to pieces.

"Did you get in trouble?"

He shook his head. "Would have been my fault anyway." He glanced across the room, toward Patrice. With a snort, he returned his attention to his plate and shoved a french fry in his mouth.

I eyed the door and wondered where Lindsay was. Was she mad enough to avoid me? Maybe I deserved to be avoided.

"Listen, since we're doing apologies, I'm sorry about the other day at the river." Jesse's last words were rushed. "I didn't mean to intrude. I . . ." He fumbled for words for a couple of seconds. "I just wanted to make sure you hadn't . . ."

"Done something stupid?"

He caught my gaze. "Yeah. People sometimes don't think clearly when they've lost someone close to them."

Jesse sounded like he knew what he was talking about. Was he talking about Patrice? Or did he mean his mother? Everyone knew Mr. Kerr had divorced Jesse's biological mom, but no one knew why. I'd never really given it any thought before. His stepmother was great; but all of a sudden, I wondered if having a stepmom take his mother's place was harder for him than it had always seemed.

I stared at him for a moment, still confused about why he was making the effort to talk. "I'm not going to hurt myself."

"Good." He held out a cup of strawberry ice cream, suddenly seeming unsure. "Want some ice cream? I'm full."

I doubted that, considering his size, but I took the ice cream anyway.

Though it was simple, something about our exchange lightened my mood. I stopped trying to figure out why he was being nice and just began to accept his efforts. My life was so surreal lately; why would this be any different? A week ago, I wouldn't have been able to imagine him acting this way. But then, I'd also never imagined there'd be a reason for him to.

Though Jesse had finished his lunch, he showed no signs of leaving. As I ate the last bites of ice cream, I tried to remember why I'd been so rude to him in the first place. It wasn't because he lived one rung up the school social ladder from me. I liked my niche, my friends. I wasn't jealous.

And as much as I wished I could blame and punish someone for Spencer's death, it wasn't Jesse's fault.

Unbidden, an image came to me of Jesse giving Spencer a high five after scoring during volleyball in PE. That solitary memory softened my attitude toward Jesse even more. Once again, I felt like Spencer was with me, guiding my actions, giving me that memory. If Jesse was making the effort to be nice to me, I should at least attempt to reciprocate.

"So, um, is the hockey team ready for the season?"

He seemed startled by the question. "I think so. Guess we better be. We have a scrimmage against Cold Creek on Saturday."

I shifted in my seat. "Good luck."

He wiped his hands on a napkin before tossing it on his tray. Then he fixed his eyes on me as he fiddled with his straw. "You should come."

It was sweet of him to ask, but I highly doubted I'd be up for any social outings anytime soon. He should know that. Still, something compelled me not to reject his suggestion entirely. "Maybe."

He nodded. There was that look of understanding again. The crazy idea that Jesse and I might become real friends startled me.

Jesse placed his hand atop mine on the table. My whole body froze, and my breathing halted.

"No pressure." He gave my hand a little squeeze. "Well, I've got to run to the library." He stood to his full height, a few inches over six feet, and grabbed his tray. "The scrimmage is at six if you decide to come."

I pried my gaze away from the scarred tabletop up to his eyes. "Okay."

After he walked away, I noticed a few people giving me curious stares. Let them look. Their guesses were as good as mine. Maybe Jesse was just a decent person, and I'd never made the effort to notice.

For all his love of books, Spencer wasn't a fan of Shakespeare. So his look of distaste wasn't a surprise when he read the Shakespeare quote the two of us had been assigned to dissect in our ninth-grade English class. He handed it to me so I could read it.

"My bounty is as boundless as the sea,
My love as deep; the more I give to thee,
The more I have, for both are infinite."
—Romeo and Juliet

CHAPTER

By the end of the day, I was totally wrung out. All I wanted to do was go home, curl up in my bed, and sleep for twelve or fourteen hours straight. If I was sleeping, I didn't have to think about Spencer's absence, Jesse's odd behavior, or Lindsay avoiding me. It was the perfect escape.

I spotted Lindsay at her locker, hurriedly shoving books into her backpack. Was she trying to get away before I saw her? I'd been sharp with her, and worst of all, I hadn't acknowledged her own pain about Spencer. Sometimes it felt as if I didn't have control of my own body or the words and emotions that spilled out of my mouth. Still, she should understand that, right?

"Linds?"

Her shoulders stiffened.

Maybe because of the stress, my anger flared more violently than usual. But I bit down on it as much as I could. "Where were you at lunch today?"

"Busy."

"Busy, where?"

She spun toward me, her eyes piercing. "Why do you

care?" she asked too loudly, drawing the attention of those around us. "You haven't cared how I feel, or how anyone else feels, for the past week."

I staggered back. "That's not fair!" But a voice inside my head acknowledged the truth of Lindsay's words. Still, I couldn't force myself to agree out loud. How could anyone be hurting as much as I was?

"It's not fair I lost a best friend, either. It's not fair that Mr. and Mrs. Isaacs lost their only child. It's not fair that Sam's wife lost her husband. None of it is fair!"

She slammed her locker loud enough that it echoed over all the post-school noise in the halls. Then she headed for the door. I stood frozen in place, stunned, until she was half-way to the exit.

"Lindsay, wait." I hurried to her side, grabbing her arm. "Come on, let's talk."

She jerked away from me. "I have to get to work."

"Work?"

Lindsay ignored my question. I gripped her arm more firmly this time and pulled her to a stop. That's when I saw the shine of tears in her eyes.

"Come on." I tugged her into the restroom. Once inside, I forced her to face me. "I'm sorry, okay?" My voice broke, and I swallowed. "I'm sorry I've been so awful. I just don't know how to deal with this. I feel like I'm being ripped to shreds."

A tear escaped Lindsay's eye. "So do I. He was my oldest friend."

The three of us always said we were best friends, but the

truth was that Linds was closer to Spencer than she was to me. I'd long ago figured out that she confessed things to him that I never heard. And that was okay then. Now, well, now I hoped things would change. They'd have to.

"I know." Tears pooled in my eyes as I took her hands in mine, examined the look of fatigue and sorrow on her face. "Something else is going on, isn't it?"

She retrieved her hands and paced to the other side of the restroom. "Everything's just gone to hell, and I want it to stop."

The way her body shook scared me. It was so unlike her, the girl who kept everything inside.

But maybe she hadn't. Maybe Spencer had been there when she'd needed to talk about whatever it was that ate at her now. I suspected it had something to do with her family.

I forced myself to be brave and selfless as I picked words I hoped would make things better. "I know I'm not Spencer, but you *can* talk to me. I'm your friend, too."

She swiped at a tear, angrily.

"Linds, is your dad home?"

She shook her head. "No. The sperm donor's gone, thank God."

I'd heard Lindsay call her father this so often it didn't faze me anymore. She maintained that the creation of her and her three brothers was the only thing Dimitri had ever done for them. He'd certainly not done anything to deserve the name *dad* or *father*. Definitely not *adax*, the Aleut word for *father*. If I knew enough to figure out he was a worthless human being, how much more had she told Spencer?

Lindsay leaned on the sink counter. "You know what else is gone?" She paused. "Our money." I could tell it tore at her to have to admit it. "I had to start work at Oregano's to help bring in some more."

Oregano's was one of only three eateries in Tundra. It was an Italian place that sat on the same small square as Chow's (the Chinese place), the Blue Walrus Bar, and most of the rest of Tundra's businesses.

Lindsay's absence during the past several days clicked into place so snugly that I couldn't believe I hadn't noticed sooner. I'd been too wrapped up in my sorrow to see that my best friend was hurting, too. And on top of her own loss, her family was facing a financial crisis.

Tears sprang to my eyes, for once not because of the friend we'd lost. He would have noticed Lindsay's situation. He wouldn't have been so self-absorbed.

"I'm sorry. I'm so, so sorry."

Lindsay pushed away from the sink. "I understand, Winter, I really do. It's just that . . ."

"You would have normally talked to Spencer about this."

She shoved her hands in her jeans' pockets and leaned against the wall. "It's just that he already knew everything, and my home life isn't something I want pasted across a bill-board, you know?"

"I'm not going to spread it around."

"It's not that I don't trust you. It's just that . . . well, Spencer found out by accident. He heard yelling . . . back when we were in first grade. . . . He saw everything. There was no going back after that. I had to fess up."

I leaned against the countertop. "What happened?"

"I missed the school bus, and Dad had to leave the Blue Walrus to come get me. Spencer was just walking out of the school when he pulled up and started yelling at me for not getting on the bus on time. 'You're so stupid,' he was shouting. Over and over, right in my face. He reeked like he'd been at the Walrus all day. Probably had been." She snorted. "Then he went back and made me sit in the truck for three hours while he drank some more."

My mouth dropped open. "I can't believe I didn't know about this." I'd known Lindsay's dad had a temper, but this was something much worse. How could I not have suspected? After all, it was Tundra, and secrets didn't stay secrets for long.

"No one did. No one except my family and Spencer. He'd seen my dad yelling at me, and I thought I'd die of embarrassment." Her face changed, reddened, as if she were reliving that long-ago day. "Dad sped away from the school that day before Spencer could say anything. I wanted to hide in a hole somewhere and never come out. But when Spencer got to the bookstore, he saw Dad's truck outside the Walrus." She stopped, swallowed hard. "He brought me a peanut butter and jelly sandwich."

My heart broke all over again, for what Lindsay had gone through and because neither of us would know the warmth of Spencer's kind heart again.

"He stayed and talked to me for a while. It may have been only a few moments, but it felt like more. After that, we talked a lot. I think I might have exploded otherwise."

I tried to ignore the hurt that she had never confided in me. She'd kept secrets from me when I'd confessed all to her. The moment I'd realized I liked Spencer as more than a friend, I'd shared it with Linds.

I hesitated, almost didn't ask the question running through my mind. But I wanted to feel closer to Lindsay— and to help her—if I could. "Why does your mom stay married to him?"

"That's what they call a dysfunctional relationship. He smacks her around; she makes up excuses for why he did it."

I should have been shocked by the revelation that Dimitri beat Anja, but I wasn't. It seemed like something he'd do. And Anja didn't come into town unless she had to, especially not when Dimitri was home from whatever temporary job he'd found somewhere away from Tundra. She stayed close to their small house, fishing, harvesting berries, and doing what she could to supplement the family's food supplies and meager income. Through necessity, Linds and her brothers had become pretty self-sufficient early on.

I wanted to hug Lindsay, to apologize again, but I sensed that wasn't what she needed. Already, I could tell she was withdrawing. She didn't like pity.

She pushed away from the wall and wiped her eyes. "I have to go. I'll call you later."

"Okay."

I didn't move as she walked toward the door. I didn't believe everything was totally healed between us, but at least she'd confided in me. She'd revealed more in the past ten minutes than she had in all the time since the second grade, when we'd become friends. I thought of that day, when she'd punched Drew Chernov in the nose for pushing me around on the playground. She'd been there for me the way Spencer had been there for her. Now it was my turn.

"Linds."

She turned halfway back toward me. "Yeah?"

"Thank you for trusting me." I wanted to say more, to tell her that she could confide anything in me, but I held back the words. She knew.

She nodded and went out the door. I waited a few moments before following. I watched her walk away, carrying too heavy a burden for someone her age. She was right. Everything was going to hell.

And I was ready for it to stop.

"Oh, I love Katherine Heigl's dress," Lindsay said as the actress arrived at the Oscars.

The fitted, red, one-shoulder Escada evoked old Hollywood. "That classic look fits her. What do you think, Spencer?" I asked, torturing him more with our girliness.

His answer? A loud, faux snore.

I hit him with a pillow from the end of the couch. He responded by grabbing me around the waist and tickling me until I screamed for mercy. When I finally freed myself, for a moment our faces were too close for me to keep the secret of how I loved him.

CHAPTER

9

Fate had decided to use me as a chew toy. Not only were Lindsay and I on new, tentative ground, but I couldn't even retreat to my room in peace when I got home.

"The Kerrs invited us over for dinner," Mom said when she stopped by my room on her way in from work.

"I'm really tired."

She leaned against the doorway to my room. "I know it's hard right now, but it's good for you to get out of this room and talk to people."

"I was in school all day. I talked to people."

Mom watched me for a moment. "I heard you and Lindsay had a disagreement."

"We talked. We're fine." At least I hoped we were. But I didn't want to go into details with my mom. It was between Lindsay and me.

She watched me for a couple of moments. "Just remember, I'm here if you want to talk."

"I know."

I went to the Kerrs' for dinner. It ended up being easier to just ride the tide than to try to get out of it. Easy, at least until I saw Jesse. It didn't matter that he said I shouldn't be embarrassed about what happened Saturday. I still was.

"Hey," he said when he came down the stairs. His dark hair, wet from a recent shower, hung to the tops of his shoulders.

"Hey." Despite our lunch conversation, I could barely meet his eyes. Now I understood more why Lindsay hated to have anyone see her raw, vulnerable side.

All throughout the meal, I couldn't shake the sense that the topics of conversation were being carefully chosen to avoid any hint of Spencer and the crash. It all felt so . . . wrong. Like it was way too soon to try to move beyond what had happened.

I forced myself to stay in my dining room chair as Jesse helped his stepmom serve dessert. Carrot cake—Spencer's favorite.

"Excuse me," I said, as I shoved my chair back and headed for the bathroom.

I'd barely closed the door behind me before the first wave of nausea hit me. I wrapped my arms around my middle and sank onto the side of the tub.

Someone knocked on the door. "Winter, honey, are you okay?" Mom asked.

I forced my voice to sound upbeat. "Yeah, be out in a minute."

I propped my elbows on my knees and let my head drop into my upturned hands. A warm touch on my shoulder caused me to jerk upright, expecting to see that Mom had slipped quietly into the bathroom.

But no one was there. A chill replaced the warmth of a moment before. I needed to go get some rest.

Not wanting to arouse sympathy, I took several deep breaths and splashed cold water on my face. When I was finished, I opened the door quietly. I expected Mom to be standing outside waiting for me, but instead I heard her and Mrs. Kerr talking in the kitchen.

As I passed the door to the garage, I noticed Jesse throwing darts. I could sneak out and go home, go back into the dining room to face the adults, or slip into the garage with Jesse. Though going home was ideal, I knew it would just cause my parents to worry.

Jesse turned slightly at my entrance, and I dreaded the inevitable question.

He held up a dart. "You play?"

That wasn't the question.

"Pretty sure the last time I threw a dart was at the spring festival when I was about ten."

He shrugged. "It's like riding a bike. You don't forget."

"Yeah, but I wasn't very good then."

He walked toward me and handed me a dart. "You can't be that bad."

Hoping to get my mind off, well, everything, I took the dart, aimed, and threw. And missed the dartboard by a good foot.

"So I was wrong. You *are* that bad."

If it wasn't already so hard to just make it through a day without breaking to pieces, I probably would have laughed. I really was terrible.

"Told you."

"Hold it like this." He held up a dart, pointing it forward between his thumb and first two fingers.

I tried to imitate his method and let another dart fly. This one came closer to the board but had less force. It stuck pitifully in the surrounding corkboard for a couple of seconds before falling out.

Jesse struggled to hide a smile.

"I think I'll go home now."

He stepped toward me with his arm extended. "Wait. Here, let me show you again." He grabbed another dart and turned me to face the dartboard. When he placed the dart in my hand, he didn't let go. Instead, he stayed behind me, lined up his view of the dartboard next to mine, and lifted my hand.

I held my breath, not because I was concentrating, but because Jesse was standing so close. He meant nothing by it, I was sure, but he was just so . . . there.

"Concentrate on the bull's-eye," he said, his breath hot on my ear. He guided my arm back. "Now just go straight forward with more strength than last time."

Strength? I had none left. Wasn't that much obvious? Still, I focused on the small red circle in the center of the dartboard. I let the dart fly, and it actually stuck in the board, two rings out from the middle.

"Hey, much better," Jesse said, still too close.

I stepped away, as casually as I could. "Guess I'm marginally less dangerous now."

When I glanced at Jesse, I caught him watching me as if

he couldn't figure something out. After a moment, he broke eye contact and sauntered over to the air-hockey table. He leaned against it, and when he looked up at me again, the perplexed look was gone.

"Sorry about dinner. I told Brenda it was too soon, but she really wanted to try to help."

I shifted my feet at the change of topic. "It's okay. It was nice of her." Even though Jesse was right. And his eerily accurate perception surprised me.

"If you want to go, I'll tell your parents you left to do homework or something."

I eyed him, trying to figure out this unexpected side of Jesse. He wasn't acting like a guy who was being nice just because his parents were forcing him to. Or because we were neighbors. And when he'd been standing behind me, it'd felt . . . I didn't know exactly how to describe it. Charged, maybe.

But that could have been my imagination, just like the warmth in the bathroom. Maybe parts of my brain were beginning to short-circuit.

"Homework is pretty far down my list."

What was wrong with me? Jesse was giving me the out I'd wanted only a few minutes before, and I wasn't taking it. But as much as I wanted to hide from the world, part of me dreaded going back to my house. What sense did it make to want to wrap myself in memories of Spencer and avoid them at the same time?

Not sure what to do, I picked up a couple of darts and practiced my aim. Jesse didn't say anything as we fell into a rhythm of taking turns throwing. He beat me every time, but I didn't care.

"It was the cake." The words tumbled down from my brain and out my mouth. I didn't know why I said it beyond the fact that it was strangely easy to talk to Jesse, even with the embarrassment still lingering.

"What?"

I took careful aim with a dart and hit the ring outside the bull's-eye. "The carrot cake earlier," I said. "It was Spencer's favorite. I made him one the day before. . . ." My voice faltered.

"The day before the crash?"

I nodded. "It was a good-luck cake." The cruel irony squeezed my heart, causing me to wince.

Jesse pitched a final dart at the board. "Life sucks sometimes," he said.

Anberlin's "Last First Kiss" started to play, and it was the final straw of the evening.

"I think I'll take you up on your offer." I stood. "Thanks."

Our eyes met. His still didn't reflect pity, but an understanding and the odd sensation that he was hiding something shone in those dark-chocolate depths.

He nodded. "See you tomorrow."

His words seemed to mean more than "I'll see you randomly in the hallway," but I pushed the thought from my mind.

I hurried out the door, leaving Jesse to explain my departure. The night was chilly, a definite sign that Labor Day had come and gone. A bright moon lit the cloudless sky, illuminating the night.

Once outside I slowed, not in any hurry to close myself up in my room, since there was no one home. I was as alone out here as I'd be inside.

I looked at the distant mountains, their peaks reflecting the moon's rays. I'd never be able to look at them again without thinking of Spencer. "I miss you," I whispered as a slight breeze brushed past me, carrying my words toward the mountains.

I sat at the wedding reception for our guidance counselor, the new Mrs. Schuler. "Here you go," Spencer said as
he handed me a paper saucer laden with cake, then a napkin
imprinted with the Schulers' names, the date of the wedding,
and a Bible verse.

I read the verse:

"I found the one my heart loves.

—Song of Solomon 3:4"

I couldn't help glancing up at Spencer and feeling the
words of the verse reaching out toward him, wondering if he'd
read it before handing me the napkin. When he caught my
gaze and smiled, I imagined he could read my mind and liked
what he saw there.

CHAPTER

Dragging myself out of bed for school on Tuesday proved no easier than it had been on Monday. I'd sat outside last night for a long time, imagining that Spencer was still with me, holding me close as we watched the stars overhead in the massive, cloudless, Alaskan sky. By the time I heard my parents leaving the Kerrs', I sighed and trudged inside, wishing I could stay in my imaginary world rather than the real one.

Unable to sleep, I'd gone downstairs to Dad's home office and stayed up late, catching up on homework. It was more for distraction than anything else, and now I was paying the price.

My classmates still gave me the same pitiful looks this morning, but those expressions didn't stop me as they had yesterday, because this time, I expected them. When I opened my locker, I glanced at Spencer's smiling face and pressed my lips together as I felt the familiar pang in my chest. God, I missed him so much. When Lindsay hadn't called last night, I'd caught myself reaching for the phone to call Spencer.

Remembering he was gone had shredded me all over again.

I hung out at my locker for a couple of minutes, hoping to see Lindsay, but she wasn't among any of the faces milling around me. With a heavy heart, I dragged myself toward first period. When I passed the library, I noticed her sitting at a table next to the windows. I considered leaving her alone—letting her come to me when she was ready—but I wanted to get back to the way we were before as quickly as possible. I missed sharing all my feelings and thoughts with her.

She glanced up as I approached her table, and a contrite look crossed her face.

"Work late last night?" I asked.

"Till closing. By the time I rode home, I was too tired to do anything but go to bed."

I slid into the chair opposite her. "You rode your bike home that late?"

She didn't really have to worry about being attacked by a human in Tundra, but a moose was a different story.

"Car's not running," she said without looking up from her notebook.

She sounded so distant, like she hadn't shared long-held secrets with me just the afternoon before. I wondered if she was regretting that, but I didn't have the courage to ask. I was afraid she'd say yes.

I searched for something to say and considered telling her about how Jesse was acting around me, but I held it in. A new weight of sorrow settled on my shoulders, this time for the chasm that had opened between Linds and me. I hoped time would heal it, because I didn't know how.

"Okay, I'll let you get back to work. See you in class."

She nodded but didn't make eye contact.

Throughout the morning, I tried to think of ways to mend our friendship. Eventually, it exhausted me and I let my mind wander. The fatigue finally won during English class, and I felt myself drifting off to sleep. Out of the corner of my eye, I saw Spencer sitting in his chair. He was alive!

I gasped, shaking myself from my trance. When I turned my head, Spencer's chair sat as empty and forlorn as it'd been the day before. And all my classmates were staring at me like I'd suddenly started speaking in Latin. When I met their gazes, most looked quickly away.

My heart hammered and my body shook as I lowered my eyes to the top of my desk. Thank goodness Mrs. Miller hadn't drawn extra attention to my embarrassing display. I stared at my textbook and tried to concentrate on the lecture.

At the end of class, I didn't meet anyone's eyes—not even Mrs. Miller's—because I was afraid she'd stop me and ask questions I didn't want to answer.

"Winter?"

I thought about pretending I didn't hear Jesse calling to me as I headed up the hall, but that would probably just draw more attention. I edged out of the flow of traffic and pasted on an everything's-fine face. "Yeah?"

"You okay?" He wore his concerned look again. His continued attention felt odd, especially when he'd barely noticed me before.

"Fine!" But I said it too cheerily, a sure sign I was anything but fine.

"What happened in there?"

I waved my hand like it was no big deal. "I didn't get much sleep last night, so I fell asleep in class. I guess I must have been dreaming or something."

He knew I was lying. I could tell by the look in his eyes.

"Okay." Someone bumped into him, causing him to step closer to me.

Instinctively, I put my hand up, and it ended up pressed against his chest. A long moment passed as our eyes met and heat flooded my face. I jerked my hand away from where it rested above his heart and barely suppressed the urge to run. Before I could flee, however, he wrapped his fingers gently around my upper arm.

"Talk to Lindsay, your mom, Mrs. Schuler. Someone." He released my arm and stepped back, giving me room to breathe.

And allowing me to meet the piercing, crackling gaze of Patrice Murray.

Spencer stared at my Halloween costume, a frothy concoction inspired by Kirsten Dunst as Marie Antoinette that had taken me five months to complete.

"Well, what do you think?"

"It's nice."

I placed my hands on my hips. "If you were any less enthusiastic, you might actually be snoring."

He turned and looked at Patrice Murray's skintight, red she-devil costume.

"I am so not wearing something like that," I said. "I'd look like a hooker." So what if mine was a little conservative, even for me.

Spencer met my eyes. "No, you'd look beautiful."

CHAPTER

11

After school, I made like a coward and hid in the restroom until most of the din of freed students faded. I stayed like that even after the quiet settled, trying to convince myself that Spencer's death hadn't irrevocably screwed up both my brain and my emotions.

Following several minutes of self-analysis, I realized I wasn't going to figure anything out sitting in an empty girls' restroom. But the time in there won me a solo walk along the path from the school—something I desperately needed.

By the time I approached the town square, however, I realized I couldn't face the idea of going home. I considered sitting in the park for a while, or possibly doing homework at the tiny Tundra Library. As I entered the square, I glanced in the window of Oregano's. Lindsay was behind the counter on the phone.

Hoping to avoid all the memories trapped in my room and hoping Linds and I could find a few minutes to patch things up some more, I stepped inside.

When Lindsay looked up and saw me, I thought maybe I'd made a mistake. I saw her expression grow more tired, her shoulders slump. But then she took a breath and gave me the hint of a smile and a small wave.

I exhaled with relief. With the loss of Spencer, I'd never been more aware of what Linds meant to me. I simply could not stand to lose my best girlfriend on the heels of losing the guy I'd given my heart to.

I took a moment to soothe my vibrating nerves. I intended to be there for Lindsay no matter how battered and empty I felt inside. I hoped I had the strength to deal with any lingering hostility she might harbor. I slid into a booth and pulled out my trig.

"You here to eat?" she asked, after finishing two orders.

I looked at her and propped my head on my upturned palm. "Don't really want to go home. Plus, it smells good in here." The smell of baking bread had always been a favorite of mine. Add the garlic, and if I closed my eyes, I could pretend I was in faraway Italy, perhaps designing costumes for some historic Roman epic.

The thought jerked me firmly back to the present. I couldn't help the shame that washed over me. Here I was, thinking about my future, when Spencer would never have his.

Lindsay must have seen my sudden change in mood, because she slid a large Coke and a hot order of cheesy garlic bread sticks onto my table. She sat beside me and leaned her head on my shoulder. "Everyone keeps telling me it'll get better someday." She sounded as if she only half believed it.

"I can't even imagine that day."

We sat in silence for a couple of minutes, watching people walking around the square.

"What happened in English today?" Lindsay asked, startling me.

I considered lying to her the way I had with Jesse, but that really wasn't the best way to repair our friendship. I swallowed against the dryness invading my throat. "I fell asleep, started dreaming. I thought I saw Spencer out of the corner of my eye, sitting in his seat. Linds, the strongest, purest joy I've ever felt shot through me."

"Until you turned around and he wasn't really there."

I nodded, unable to verbalize the despair I'd then experienced.

"I have to go to the bathroom," Lindsay said, after a pause. "Can you catch the phone if it rings?"

"Sure."

When she was gone, I took two more to-go orders and seated a trio of tourists.

When Lindsay returned to the front counter, her normally dark complexion looked pale.

"Are you okay?"

"Just need to eat something," she said.

"You can't keep skipping lunch."

"I know," she said a little testily, then caught herself. "I just need some time to settle into the new schedule, that's all."

She was holding something back again, but I didn't want to push too hard.

As the evening wore on, the restaurant grew busier and busier.

"I don't want you to ride home this late," I said, while

Linds finally helped Casey Stone, the restaurant's owner, close three hours later. "Just stay at my house tonight."

I thought she might refuse at first, but instead, she nodded. After she called her mom, we headed home.

Once we'd both finished the last of our homework, eaten a late-night snack of orange sherbet, and slipped into bed, I stared at the ceiling and listened to Lindsay's breathing. I could tell, from its rhythm, that she was still awake.

"Do you have nightmares?" she asked.

I didn't have to ask the kind she meant. "Every night. I wake up crying every single night."

A few more seconds ticked by.

"I'm sorry I've been so harsh," she said. "Guess I have more of the sperm donor's genetics than I'd like to admit."

I turned toward her. "Why do you say that?"

"I lash out at the people who mean the most to me."

"It's hard, Linds. Too hard." I bit my lip as thoughts of Spencer—his laugh, his smile, his teasing—flooded me.

"Yeah."

She was quiet for so long that my eyes drifted closed.

"You know, he was jealous when you and I became friends."

My eyes popped back open. "Really? Why?"

"Because he thought if I had a girl best friend, I wouldn't be friends with him anymore." She uttered a half-amused, half-heartbroken laugh. "Stupid boy."

I smiled, despite the ache in my own chest. "I guess I was stupid, too. Part of me was always jealous of the time you two had before I knew him. Of the closeness I knew the two of you shared without me."

Linds looked toward me for the first time. "Guess we were the stupid trio then, because when you started having non-friend feelings for him, I was so afraid if you got together, he'd be different with me. I was terrified he wouldn't be there anymore, and I'd truly be alone."

"You knew him, Linds. He'd never do that."

She placed her lower arm across her forehead and looked at the ceiling again. "I wanted to believe that, but . . ."

She'd had a lot of experience with people letting her down. I reached over and squeezed her hand. "I'm here."

She squeezed back and didn't let go. We lay in silence until her breathing finally slowed. I continued to stare at the ceiling, hoping that my despair wouldn't cause me to hurt her again.

His lips lowered, closer, closer. I could taste their combination of sweet and salty, feel their moist warmth, before they even made contact with my own.

Something shook me so hard that his face blurred before me, then disappeared. I whimpered as I reached for him.

"Winter, wake up."

I jerked, coming awake with a gasp, shocked that the very real images and feelings had only been a dream.

"You were dreaming, thrashing around," Lindsay said as she looked down at me with a questioning look on her face.

God, what had I said?

"Another nightmare?"

I rubbed my face, trying to wake up more and form a coherent response, a lie. "I guess. I can't remember."

"Really? Nothing? Dreams usually linger for a little bit when you wake up."

"No, nothing," I said, hoping she would attribute my testiness to being abruptly awakened. "Maybe you shook it out of me."

She slipped from the bed and went to the bathroom, leaving me to obsess about the dream now burned into my memory. To wonder again about my sanity. I sat up on the side of the bed and ran my fingers through my tangled hair. That's how my thoughts felt—tangled.

"You said Jesse's name in your sleep," Lindsay said, when she walked out of the bathroom.

"Really?" I scrunched my forehead as if I was trying to remember, then shook my head, all while panic surged through me. She couldn't find out what I'd really been dreaming. I didn't even want to remember it, because it was all kinds of wrong.

That kind of dream, one that left me warm and breathless, should be about Spencer. Guilt and shame washed over me, punishing me for my betrayal.

I stood. "Don't know what to tell you. Just wish I could forget *all* my dreams like that."

I walked past her, closing myself in the bathroom. I tried to force myself to forget the dream. To forget how Jesse had held me and how much I'd enjoyed it. But no matter how much I tried, it didn't work. If anything, it made the images clearer in my mind.

I stayed in the bathroom longer than necessary, hoping Linds would fall back asleep. But the effort was for nothing. She sat in my leather chair when I returned to the bedroom.

"Is something going on?" she asked.

"What do you mean?"

"With Jesse?"

"No! How could you ask me that? You know I love Spencer." I choked on his name, sank onto the edge of the bed and hugged my pillow close.

"I know. I'm sorry." She looked ashamed for asking, making me feel horrible for misleading her. "It's just that Monica saw you two in the hallway yesterday, talking kind of close."

"He just saw what happened in English and asked if I was okay."

"When you thought you saw Spencer?"

I nodded. "I didn't tell him that, though. I said I'd just fallen asleep in class and woke up suddenly."

"Seems odd of him to ask you. It's not like you two were ever close friends."

"Not really *that* odd. We live next door to each other, and our parents are good friends. I'm sure his parents have asked him to keep an eye on me. I mean, you saw him the day of the cookout. I don't think me running into him put us on the fast track to bosom buddy-dom."

Did she honestly think I could replace Spencer so quickly? Ever?

The dream was just one of those crazy, random collections of images that made no sense once you left REM. That was all.

I would not focus on the fact that my body was still humming as a result of it.

Wonderful smells of freshly baked yeast rolls, succulent turkey, and yummy pumpkin pie wafted through our dining room as everyone around the table—my family, Spencer's, and Lindsay and her youngest brother—took turns saying what they were thankful for.

"Your turn, Spencer," my dad said.

"I'm thankful for two best friends," Spencer said.

Was it my imagination, or did he hold my gaze longer than normal?

CHAPTER

12

Avoiding Jesse ended up being harder than I'd expected. This was one time I wished I went to one of those big high schools—the kind that held as many people as Tundra's entire population. Much easier to hide from the star of your hot and totally inappropriate dream.

The past couple of days, I'd taken my lunch from home and eaten sitting on the bleachers in the gym. In the classes we shared, I timed my arrivals and departures before his. I firmly pushed memories of the dream, my breakdown in the backyard, him carrying me to my bedroom, and the dart lesson from my mind.

Still, I was jumpy anytime someone approached me from behind. How would I be able to face Jesse without my anxiety betraying me? I didn't want him getting the wrong idea. Because I didn't like him that way. I still longed for Spencer. A part of me still held out hope that the past couple of weeks had been a horrible mistake and he'd be found holed up on the mountain somewhere.

When I opened my locker after my last class on Thursday,

a folded note fell down from behind the taped photos inside the door.

Since I expected it to be from Lindsay, my breath caught when I recognized Spencer's handwriting.

"Hey. Want to grab a bite after school? S."

I gripped the edge of my locker and scanned the faces as they flocked toward the exit, praying I'd see the one I thought I'd lost forever.

"Winter, what's wrong?"

I hadn't even noticed Lindsay stepping up next to me. I couldn't speak, so I handed her the note.

Her face grew darker as she read. "Is this someone's idea of a joke? I will totally beat the crap out of them."

"Look at it, Linds. That's Spencer's handwriting."

She examined it more closely before looking at me. Sadness crept into her eyes as she shifted her gaze to the inside of my locker. "It must have gotten stuck behind one of your pictures."

"Yeah. It fell down when I opened the door."

"Winter, I mean, it got stuck there . . . before."

She might as well have punched me in the chest. Feeling my grip on reality waver, I spun back to face my locker. "Yeah. Of course."

I heard the words she didn't say. Spencer was gone, and he wasn't coming back. Why did part of me refuse to believe that?

When I accompanied Lindsay to Oregano's that afternoon, she didn't comment on my presence there. She simply accepted that this was how it would be. Casey seemed to accept it, too.

At least she didn't seem to mind when I stepped in for Lindsay from time to time. I guessed this was one of those things that people thought would keep my mind off Spencer's death. And for a minute or two here and there, it did.

But sometimes, during lulls, the loss hit me as real and sharp as it'd been the night my dad had come home with the news of death written on his face.

"Have you seen them?" I asked Lindsay as we walked out onto the square Friday evening. When she looked at me, I nodded toward Tundra Books.

"Nothing beyond noticing them go in and out of the store."

I should have been visiting Spencer's parents, but I just couldn't. I wasn't ready. I doubted it would do them any good to see me break down in front of them.

Another week passed. I wasn't the person I'd been before Spencer's death, and probably never would be again, but at least my parents had stopped looking at me like I might shatter. My classmates had stopped staring, and miraculously I'd been able to avoid Jesse. I still caught myself sinking into thoughts of Spencer more often than not, watching out the windows as if he might suddenly walk into view. Rereading the snippets of prose and poetry he'd written.

All the time I was spending with Lindsay made me aware that something else was gnawing at her. I didn't ask her about it for a few days, hoping she would eventually open up. I suspected it had something to do with her father again, but I hated the idea of bringing him up in conversation. Maybe she still wasn't ready to be totally open with me like she had been with Spencer.

I waited to broach the topic until Oregano's dinner traffic quieted one night, and she slid into the booth opposite me with a bowl of tortellini.

"Tell me what's wrong."

She didn't deny it, simply sat staring into her bowl as she stirred the pasta in circles.

"Just dreading the inevitable talk with Coach Stevak. I'm quitting the team."

"Quitting? Why?"

She raised her eyebrows at me and motioned around the restaurant. "Hello, I have a job."

"I can fill in when you have practice or games. I'm here anyway."

"You're here when I'm here."

"I'm here because . . . it doesn't remind me of Spencer." I took a deep breath and tried to put on a happier face. "Plus, I think I can manage the starving hordes for a couple of hours." As if Tundra could have a single horde, let alone multiple.

"Winter—"

I held up my hand. "So what if Casey lets me pour drinks and take orders because she feels sorry for me. I don't care. Let me do this for you." I looked down and fiddled with the edge of my notebook. "You love basketball. I don't want you to give it up." She deserved to have one thing in her life that fate hadn't stomped beneath its heavy boot.

She eyeballed me for a moment before smiling. "Thank you."

"You're welcome." I finished my last trig problem before I asked my next question. "How's your mom?"

"The same. She got a few days' work cooking on a salvage boat. The latest batch of bruises has nearly cleared up." She said it so matter-of-factly that my heart ached for her. But in a strange way, I was glad she was so forthright. It was the first time she'd said anything else about her family since the day of our fight, and her words now gave me hope that she was going to continue to confide in me.

When I saw movement on the sidewalk outside, we both looked out the window. Drew Chernov and Brock Robertson strolled by. Drew looked at Lindsay and gave her a smug smile and a two-fingered salute.

"Asshole," she said, plain enough that he had to have heard. He laughed and kept walking.

"Um, am I missing something?"

"No. You know he's a jerk."

"True, but I'm sensing a new level of jerkiness." Beyond the stupid, juvenile grudge he still held from our elementary school days. He was one of those guys who didn't take well to being publicly punched by a girl.

She sat back and propped her feet on the other end of my side of the booth.

"The first night I was working here, Drew came in with Brock and some other guys." She paused. "Caleb was with them. He seems nice, and I actually began to think I might have a chance with him the way he kept watching me." A dreamy look softened the stress I'd seen on her face a lot lately. "He has a beautiful smile."

I bit down on my desire to ask her why she hadn't told me about this development with Caleb sooner. "You like him a lot."

The dreaminess fell away. "Yeah, but I don't think it matters."

"Did he say something?" Maybe this time I could punch a guy for *her*.

"No. Drew did."

"What?"

"I guess he noticed Caleb looking at me, so he said, 'You don't want to get involved with her. Her family's messed up, poor as dirt. Dad's a loser drunk. I'm surprised they let her work here at all—her dad got arrested here a year ago.'"

A flush of anger heated my face, and my fingers curled around the edge of my textbook. "I feel the need to do bodily harm." I realized it was one of the first times I'd felt anything but sorrow and embarrassment since before Labor Day.

"We tried that once, remember? Didn't seem to do any good. Do have to say it took all my self-control not to slug him, or at least pour his drink in his lap." She shrugged. "But I need the job. And the kicker is, it was all true."

"Linds."

She met my gaze. "You know it is. And it's getting worse. Dad *is* a loser. At least he used to manage to bring home a little money, now he's just drinking it all. He came home stone-cold broke this time, even had the balls to ask Mom for money."

I knew from the look of disgust on her face that her mom had given it to him. "That's why you're working? What about Ryan and David?" I hadn't seen her older brothers in weeks, and then only in passing at the grocery.

"They're working odd jobs, raising enough to head down

to Dutch Harbor. Try to get on some crab boats for king crab season. Mom hates the idea of them going out, but it's not like money's floating down the Naknek."

I might not understand Anja Kusagak's views on many things, but her fear for her sons made sense. Especially since crab fishing on the Bering Sea was the deadliest job in the world.

Freddie McClain came in the front door, looking hungry after a day of working as the solo employee of the borough's road department.

Though Lindsay tried to shake off our conversation with her usual that's-just-the-way-it-is attitude, I could tell she was bruised. Of course, losing a close friend was the worst of it, but I thought Drew's comment in front of Caleb ranked high on the disappointment ladder. She'd become used to her dad's behavior; so that, she could handle. But she'd hoped for a chance with Caleb.

If Drew walked back by outside, I was so going to deck him. And with all the anger and hurt seething within me, I might not stop punching.

I looked out toward the empty block of Town Park. Such a short time ago, my only worries had been about how to follow my dream of being a costume designer and how I was going to tell Spencer I liked him as more than a friend. How quickly things had changed.

Now life seemed heavier, darker and overflowing with bigger concerns. Ones bigger than Alaska itself. Ones I couldn't fix.

I stared out the window of Chow's as I stuffed another bite of black-pepper chicken into my mouth. Jesse Kerr and Patrice Murray stepped out of Tundra Books.

"Since when are they customers?"

Spencer shrugged. "Maybe he was getting her a Christmas present."

I snorted. "Patrice? A book?"

"We sell things besides books, you know."

"Oh, yes, Jesse must have bought her a romantic coffee mug full of beans."

"Be nice. Jesse's a good guy."

"Just hasn't found the right girl?"

He looked back at me. "Something like that."

CHAPTER 13

I would never go to the Snow Ball.

On a Monday morning five weeks after the crash, this realization hit me full in the face.

Between my locker and my first-period classroom sat a table at which Patrice Murray and Skyler Thornby, both class officers, were signing up volunteers for the formal dance.

The pain felt like a red-hot sword had been shoved through my heart and out my back. I couldn't breathe, no matter how hard I fought to suck down air.

God, I would never dance with Spencer. Never see him again. It hit me so strongly that it reawakened a part of me that had turned numb. I swung around and hurried in the opposite direction, trying in vain to outrun the horror of the truth. As I careened around the corner that led toward the gym, I ran into someone so hard that both of our books went flying.

"Damn it!" I dropped to the floor without even seeing who I'd plowed into. "I'm sorry."

"It's okay."

I looked up to find myself eye to eye with Jesse. Of all the people to hit. Why couldn't it have been Drew Chernov? I'd have loved to have broken one of his bones in the process.

"I'm sorry. I wasn't looking where I was going." I gathered his books into a pile.

"It's okay, really." He smiled, a teasing smirk. "Though I do have to wonder if I've done something in particular to make you keep running into me."

My face flushed. "I'm just clumsy. I didn't mean to, either time." I felt myself begin to babble, and I became more desperate to escape. I hated myself for automatically remembering the dream I'd had about him.

Jesse placed his hand on my upper arm. "Stop apologizing. It's no big deal."

I nearly choked on a gasp and quickly stood, breaking the contact with Jesse. I was losing my mind. That was the only excuse for what had felt like a zing of awareness—guy-girl awareness—when he'd touched me. I couldn't like him. I didn't. I loved Spencer. Always had, always would.

"What's wrong?"

I shook my head and wondered if I could zip past him without letting him see how much his nearness unnerved me. "Nothing."

He sighed and leaned his forearm against the bank of lockers. "You know, I may be a jock, but I'm not stupid. I know you've been avoiding me for some reason, and I know something has you upset."

I let out a long breath and leaned back against the lockers. "I've just been trying to avoid things that remind me of Spencer, and it's impossible." I knew I sounded on the verge of tears, but I couldn't help it. Just when I thought I might get through a day with some semblance of peace, something punched me with sorrow again.

He waited for a moment, like he was debating saying whatever was on his mind. "What was it this time?"

I looked up at the white ceiling tiles in an effort to stave off the coming tears. "Patrice and Skyler signing up volunteers for the Snow Ball."

"You and Spencer were supposed to go?"

I nodded.

"I know this might sound trite, but try not to think about it. A lot can happen in two months."

I don't know which surprised me more, Jesse's use of the word "trite" or what felt like a hidden meaning in his words. Against my better judgment, I looked up into his dark eyes and felt something there, just beyond the surface. I broke eye contact and glanced in the direction of Lindsay, who was standing ten yards away.

Confusion and a touch of betrayal showed on her features. Crap, just what I needed, to put Linds and myself at odds again. Was this day cursed?

"I gotta go. Sorry again for running you over."

"If you apologize again, I'm going to have to think of an appropriate punishment."

His teasing startled me enough that I nearly tripped over my own feet as I pushed away from the lockers. I didn't respond. I didn't know how to.

Lindsay stood her ground as I approached.

"I thought you said nothing was going on between you two."

I stopped and gave her an exasperated look. "There's not." Even if there were strange currents flowing between us, ones I couldn't attribute to him being nice to me at his parents' suggestion. "In my apparent desire to be the clumsiest person on earth, I came around the corner and ran right into him again."

"And this led to a deep conversation in the hallway?"

"Linds, I don't know what you think is going on, but he just asked how I was doing. He was just being nice."

"Since when does Jesse Kerr give a crap?"

"Apparently since he saw me pass out, when I heard Spencer's body was either incinerated or eaten by a bear." I said it too loudly. A few people nearby stopped, gasped, stared.

A hand at my back made me jump, and for a crazy moment I thought it was Spencer coming to make peace between his two best friends. But the tall, imposing presence of Jesse stepped into the space between Linds and me and the rest of the students in the corridor. He placed a broad hand on Lindsay's shoulder.

"I don't think you want to have this conversation out here," he said. He gently guided us toward the empty gym.

Lindsay was still so stunned by my revelation that she let him.

Once inside, Lindsay took several unsteady breaths. Then she looked at me with haunted eyes. I could no longer hold the tears. They streaked down my cheeks. "I'm sorry. I shouldn't have said that."

"I knew . . ." She cleared her throat. "I knew they couldn't find the body, but . . . God, Winter, it's too awful to even think about." She ran her fingers into her hair, pressing the heels of her hands against her temples as if she could squeeze the image out of her mind.

I sank onto an old, scarred bleacher, too tired to stand anymore. I glanced over and noticed Jesse standing by the door like a sentinel.

Lindsay looked at him, and he met her gaze. "I'm sorry," she said.

"It's okay. I know it's tough." He glanced at me before returning his attention to the hallway outside the door, letting Lindsay and me work this out between us.

The bleachers squeaked as Lindsay sank down beside me. "I'm sorry. I don't know what's wrong with me."

I caught her hand in mine. "A lot has happened lately. None of it's fair." I swiped the tears off one of my cheeks. "Linds, I need you right now, and I know you don't like to admit you need anyone, but I think you need me, too. I don't want to fight anymore or to defend myself. I need to be able to say and do whatever I have to in order to get through this, even though most days that seems impossible. And I want you to be able to talk to me about whatever." I paused, considering my next words, wondering if I should say them. "Talk to me, not accuse me."

She bristled, but then I saw her force herself to relax before she nodded. "I can't get the image out of my head."

"I know. I keep having nightmares about it." I exhaled slowly. "I wish I hadn't said that. You shouldn't have to live with the image, too."

Lindsay glanced past me to where Jesse was doing a good job of pretending he wasn't there.

"Why was he there when you fainted?"

"He came with his parents. The Kerrs were talking to Mom and Dad when I woke up. They all thought I was still asleep. But when I heard Dad talk about what he and the rescue crew found, the whole world spun and went black." I considered telling her about how Jesse had carried me to bed, but despite my assertion that we needed to be honest with each other, I didn't think now was the best time to bring it up.

Lindsay shook her head. "Seems like nothing makes sense anymore."

I knew how she felt.

The warning bell for first period rang. Lindsay stood. "I've got a test. Can't be late."

I could almost see the shutting-down part of herself so she could do what had to be done. She'd deal with the new knowledge about Spencer. I wished I could compartmentalize like that. That image, the continued expectation that I'd see Spencer around every corner, my too-heavy heart—these things followed me around every minute of every day.

Lindsay nodded at Jesse as she left the gym. Not wanting to draw any more attention to myself by being late to class, I followed. But when I came up next to Jesse, I stopped. I looked up at him, tried to figure out this guy I thought I'd had pegged years ago.

"Thank you."

He smiled, and I had to admit that he had a beautiful smile, one that made me want to believe, suddenly, that things would be okay. "Anytime."

That single word followed me all the way to class.

"Dang, it's cold!" I grabbed another blanket off the back of the couch, trying to ignore the wicked sound of the wind whistling around our house. Outside, winter was in full force. I might be Alaskan, but even I got bone cold sometimes.

"Come here, wuss," Spencer said as he pulled me close to him.

It wasn't anything abnormal for us to cuddle up on the couch. He wrapped his arm around my shoulders and returned his attention to the movie. I stared at the screen, but nothing registered beyond my desire to wrap my arms around Spencer and confess all of my hidden feelings.

CHAPTER

14

"How did the test go?" I asked as Lindsay got into the lunch line behind me. I wanted to avoid heavy conversation, so I'd been focusing on surface topics.

"Fine, I think. But when I'll ever use physics, I have no idea."

"Precisely why I didn't take it."

"It was that or choir, and you know I don't sing."

"Not without making dogs howl, anyway."

She smacked me on the shoulder, and for a moment, it felt like old times. But Spencer's gaping absence kept the spurts of normalcy to a minimum.

Lindsay cursed as she searched her purse.

"What's wrong?"

"My wallet isn't in here. Crap, I think I left it on the bed this morning."

I opened my mouth to say I'd buy her lunch and she could pay me back, but I didn't get the chance.

"I've got it." Caleb Moore extended a five-dollar bill past us to Cheryl Sturgeon, the cashier.

Already, Lindsay was shaking her head. "I can't let you do that."

He smiled wide, one of those smiles that stops females of all ages in their tracks, stunning them into blabbering idiocy. "I already did."

Caleb winked at Linds, and for a moment, I thought she might melt.

"I'll pay you back tomorrow."

"No need. Not every day I get to buy a pretty girl lunch."

Oh, he was smooth. I eyed him, trying to figure out if it was genuine. I glanced past him to Drew Chernov, and red flags went up. The company Caleb was continuing to keep was less than ideal.

Drew narrowed his eyes at me. "Hurry up. Some of us are hungry."

Jackass. "Bite me," I said.

Okay, that felt normal, too. Weird. As I grabbed my tray and led Lindsay away before she started drooling on herself, I realized that Drew was the first person who'd treated me carelessly since Spencer's crash. Well, there'd been that less-than-happy look from Patrice the day she'd seen Jesse and I talking in the hall, but Drew was the first one to open his piehole and be an all-out jerk. In a very odd way, I was glad. Still didn't mean I liked him. They'd be wearing bikinis in January in Fairbanks before *that* happened.

I'd noticed Linds stealing glances at Caleb every day, but I'd chosen to ignore it. Partly because I hadn't had much to give in the past few weeks, and partly because he hadn't stood up for her when Drew had opened his fat, idiotic mouth.

When we slid into chairs at our usual table, I saw her looking back toward where Caleb was taking a seat with Drew and some of the other charter members of the popular crowd.

"The crush isn't going away, is it?"

She sighed and shoved her lima beans around on her plate. "No. I wish it would. But every time I see him, my heart rate doubles and I get all jittery."

I knew that feeling well. I rode out a familiar wave of pain before I spoke again.

"Can't say I like some of his crowd, but he seems nice." I hoped anyway. Maybe if Linds found someone, at least she could start to heal from our loss. "Maybe just talk to him, act like the scene with Drew never happened."

"Yeah, because that's all kinds of easy."

I shrugged, because I didn't have a better solution or, honestly, any energy for matchmaking. Lindsay deserved to be happy, and if Caleb Moore could make her happy, I was all for it. But our short conversation about him was about all I could stand without memories of Spencer rendering me useless.

The need to strike out still roiled inside of me. I wanted someone to pay for something. The bark of Drew's laughter across the cafeteria gave me the perfect target. When Lindsay glanced away, I closed my milk carton and slid it into a side pocket of my bag.

"I've got to run to the restroom. See you later." I stood with my tray.

"Okay. See you in history."

I forced myself to maintain a casual demeanor as I dumped my tray and left the room. I walked down the hall and turned the corner that led to Drew's locker. A quick scan in each direction revealed I was alone, so I retrieved the milk and poured it through the slats in the top of the locker. I hoped he wouldn't visit it until the milk got nice and stinky.

For the first time in weeks, I really smiled.

"I see your mom decided to increase the number of love quotes this year," I said as I stepped inside Tundra Books. Quotes hung from or were tacked to every available surface.

"She swore it increased sales last February," Spencer replied. "What do you think? Will this make people buy more romance and relationship books?" He extended a piece of white pasteboard toward me.

I took it and read the quote:

"Nobody has ever measured, not even poets, how much a heart can hold. —Zelda Fitzgerald"

I looked up at him and said, "Quotes do help people say what they can't themselves."

CHAPTER

15

"*Name* the three groups of Southeastern Coastal Indians," I said from my spot in the worn, red corner booth at Oregano's.

Lindsay didn't pause as she refilled the Parmesan containers on the tables. "Tlingit, Haida, and Tsimshian."

I consulted my study notes as we prepared for the next day's test in Alaskan history and culture. "Who founded the first permanent Russian settlement on Kodiak Island?"

"Grigory Shelikhov." She snapped the Parmesan container closed. "Murdering bastard."

I winced. But Shelikhov had, in fact, murdered hundreds of indigenous Koniag in order to establish Russian dominance on the island. Similar story as the one for the Lower 48, just different white guys coming from a different direction.

"Have you studied for the essay portion yet?"

Lindsay moved on to refilling napkin containers. "Some. I think I'll be okay. Comes pretty easy to me."

History was her favorite subject. She did well in it without really trying. She had a good chance of following in my sister Kristen's footsteps to become a history teacher. That would certainly put her several notches above the rest of her family on the ambition scale.

"So, I have a question for you." Lindsay stopped her tasks and leaned one hand against the booth across from me. "Any idea how milk got in Drew Chernov's locker?"

"I think I tripped as I was walking down that particular hallway consuming my daily vitamin D."

She barked out a laugh, the first I'd heard in weeks, and wrapped me in a crushing hug.

The ringing of the phone allowed me to breathe normally again. I studied my notes as Lindsay took someone's order. Learning the names and dates and facts, which I'd always found interesting, held less appeal than it used to. Most things did. I thought of the untouched sketch pad on my desk, then refocused on my notes, trying to keep the image at bay.

"So, next question," Lindsay said as she slid onto the end of the booth opposite me.

Before I could formulate a question, the front door opened. In walked Caleb Moore, alone. Lindsay slid out of the booth without looking to see who'd entered. When she saw Caleb, she started and turned to me. Her eyes had gone huge, and her body tensed. A sure sign she had it bad—nothing typically freaked her out like this.

"Calm down," I said under my breath so Caleb couldn't hear me. "Just treat him like any other customer."

"Not that many hot customers come through the front door," she hissed back at me before heading to the front counter.

True. Freddie McClain had passed up hot a long time ago—if he'd even ever been hot in the first place.

"Hey," Caleb said with a smile.

"Hey."

I hoped only I could hear the tremor in Lindsay's voice because I knew her so well.

"What can I get you?"

His smile grew wider, and I'd swear I could see a blush beneath Lindsay's dark skin tone.

"I'll take an order of bread sticks and a Coke."

Hmm, didn't sound like a big, dinner-type order. Was it just an excuse to come in and see Lindsay? Did he regret how he'd allowed Drew to steer him away from her? If so, I had to give the boy some credit. Maybe by being new in town, he'd just needed time to figure out the lay of the land socially.

I tried not to be too obvious about staring as Lindsay wrote down Caleb's order and called it back to Casey.

I watched Caleb's face. He did have a nice smile, and his eyes seemed kind.

"I couldn't work here," he said as he leaned against the counter. "I'd be as big as a house."

Lindsay quirked her eyebrow. "Somehow I doubt that."

He leaned forward. "Maybe I should see if I can get hired on. Then we'd see who's right."

Lindsay nearly spilled the Coke she'd poured.

Caleb chuckled. "You okay?"

"Yes." Lindsay, poor thing, wasn't very convincing. She couldn't even bring her eyes up to meet his.

Caleb, however, didn't take his eyes off Lindsay. I was surprised the undercurrent wasn't visible. If nothing else, I believed he was genuinely attracted to Linds.

If Drew got anywhere near the restaurant in the next few minutes, I'd tackle him and drag him across Town Park by his nostrils.

I caught Casey's eye as she prepared the order, and she gave me one of those raised-eyebrow looks.

Caleb took a sip of his drink but still didn't take his eyes away from Lindsay, even when she had to pause to take another order.

"I thought of something else I want," he said the moment she hung up the phone.

"Okay." She reached for the order pad.

Caleb placed his hand over hers. "You won't need that."

I held my breath, and I'm pretty sure so were Lindsay and Casey.

"Oh?" Lindsay said.

"I'd like to take you out for dinner sometime."

"Oh," she said again, disbelieving.

"What do you say?"

Lindsay opened her mouth, and for a few seconds, she looked like a fish out of water. She glanced at me, and I found myself nodding.

"Sure."

"Chow's, tomorrow night?"

This time, Lindsay smiled. And I saw a joy in her dark eyes that I'd never seen. It made me sad and happy at the same time.

"Sounds nice," she said.

"Great. I'll pick you up around six."

Panic flared on Lindsay's face, and I knew what she was thinking. She didn't want Caleb to see her meager home, which sat above the confluence of the Naknek River and Pebble Creek.

"How about we meet there?"

Caleb, agreeing, didn't seem to notice anything strange.

By the time he left, I was about to combust.

Lindsay waited until Caleb walked across the park and disappeared before bouncing back to our booth.

"Oh my God! He just asked me out!"

I saw the look of worry mixing with her excitement—worry that this would hurt me. Just because I felt Spencer's loss had left a hole where my heart should be didn't mean my best friend couldn't move on and find a shred of happiness.

"I know. I heard."

"Eavesdropper."

I let out a laugh. "Tell me where I could be in this building and *not* hear what you said."

She met my eyes. "Is this okay with you?"

It took all the willpower I could muster to keep the pain from showing on my face. I pushed the idea of the dates that never were back into the recesses of my mind. "Of course it's okay. I'm happy for you." I just hoped it didn't end in heartbreak for her. "Of course, if he hurts you, I'll have to run him over with a snowmobile this winter."

She smiled at me, and that joy I'd glimpsed seemed to glow within her.

"You know," Casey said from the doorway into the kitchen. "If I were a decade younger, I'd give you a run for your money. I feel like a dirty old woman saying it, but that boy is not bad to look at."

"Good thing you *are* old," Lindsay teased her.

"Careful, missy, or I'll dock your pay for being a smart mouth. Or for flirting on the clock."

Lindsay made a dramatic show of covering her mouth. Casey, who was only about thirty and very pretty in a natural way, rolled her eyes and returned to the kitchen. "Good thing I've got a hot date with a pilot from Dillingham tomorrow night," she said over her shoulder.

No longer able to concentrate on studying, I watched as Lindsay waited on two couples I didn't recognize. Probably tourists staying upriver at the Brown Bear Lodge. They smiled, Lindsay smiled. Everyone looked happy to be alive—and happy to be part of a couple.

I swallowed hard and looked out the window at the darkness cloaking Tundra. I imagined Spencer walking out of the darkness. But no matter how long I stared out into the night, he didn't appear.

I stopped in the middle of the school hallway and laughed. Spencer stood with his arms outstretched, showing off a long-sleeved white tee with a green leprechaun pursing his lips and the words "Kiss me, I'm Irish" emblazoned across the chest.

"What, not going to take me up on it?" he teased.

I pushed past him, wishing I had the nerve to surprise him with a monster lip lock. Instead, I kept my tone light and teasing like his. "Maybe if you actually were Irish."

"Not even a peck on the cheek?" he asked as he followed me.

Not even a peck on the cheek, because I would want so much more.

CHAPTER

16

After finishing my homework and chores on Saturday, I retreated to my room, feeling tired and restless at the same time. The low clouds and lessening of the daylight hours didn't help my mood. How was I going to make it through the darkness of winter?

I stared at my sketch pad but dismissed the idea of picking it up. I hadn't felt a speck of inspiration since August. My hand didn't itch to wrap around a drawing pencil like it used to. Maybe that dream had died along with Spencer.

Other than textbooks, I hadn't read anything in a month. So I sank down in front of my bookshelves and scanned the titles. I pulled Dana Stabenow's *A Deeper Sleep* off the shelf. I ran my fingers over the title and tried not to think of Spencer. Even so, I opened the cover to the page where I knew I'd see his familiar handwriting.

"I think Kate Shugak is hot!"

I snorted, even as tears blurred my vision. He'd always teased me by saying some character, some actress, some singer was hot. As I looked back, I wondered if it had all been his careful attempt at flirting, to see how I'd react to him expressing interest in another woman, real or imagined.

"Oh, Spencer." I closed the book and started to slide it back into its place between A *Taint in the Blood* and *Whisper to the Blood*. But a bookmark fell out of it into my lap—a bookmark I'd never seen before.

I picked it up and noticed a quote in script.

"Where there is great love, there are always miracles. —Willa Cather"

Was this a sign?

I got to my feet and paced the room. At the window, I stopped and looked toward the imposing mountains. Was Spencer really dead, and his spirit lingering? Or was he still up there and somehow, crazily, our bond was strong enough that he could reach out to me?

Or was I losing my grip on reality?

I slid down the wall to the carpet and stared at the bookshelf. The bookmark was just a coincidence. Or had Spencer slipped it into the book when I'd bought it, thinking I'd find it and figure out how he felt? My heart ached that I'd not seen it until now, when it was too late. That the bookmark, like the note in my locker, had stayed hidden until its appearance could stab me with grief.

I ran my hands back over my ponytail and stared at the bookshelf, restraining myself from leafing through every book in the hope of finding other hidden messages from Spencer.

All those books had held hours of enjoyment. They'd each been the topics of conversations between Spencer and myself. That's why reading still held too much of Spencer for me to enjoy the stories now. I doubted even new books would carry me away.

Plus, I didn't think I was ready to step foot in Tundra Books yet. I feared breaking down, and his parents didn't need that. I'd seen them around town some, but I hadn't been able to force myself to speak to them even though they were like second parents to me. I wondered if they felt the same, because I knew they'd seen me on more than one occasion since the memorial service.

Why couldn't a broken heart heal as fast as a broken bone?

I flopped back on the thick red carpet—which I'd wanted because it reminded me of those Hollywood red carpets—and stared at the white expanse of my ceiling. I couldn't even go to Lindsay's to hang out, because she was off hiking with Caleb. Seemed the boy liked nature photography, so they'd hit the trail along the river to find subject matter.

If only I had something to do that had no ties to Spencer. Hard to find in a small town like Tundra, when so much of my life had been touched by him.

As my mind wandered aimlessly, Jesse's invitation to the hockey scrimmage floated to the front of my thoughts. I'd skipped it, of course. But the fact that the team had a game against Homer today wound its way up from wherever my brain had stored this information. Hockey definitely didn't bring Spencer immediately to mind—even though he was never far from the front of my thoughts. Maybe the game would allow me to escape, if only for a few minutes. I could always leave and do something else.

What, I didn't know.

I raised myself from the floor and pulled on a University of Alaska sweatshirt and a pair of blue Chucks. Not exactly a red carpet outfit, but there weren't any red carpets at Tundra Ice Rink.

When I went downstairs and grabbed my jacket off the back of the couch, Mom eyed me from where she was preparing a casserole in the kitchen.

"Going somewhere, sweetie?"

"Thought I'd drop in on the hockey game."

"Sounds fun. I hear they're good this year." She didn't make a big deal out of my going, and I was grateful.

The difference in temperature between the inside of the house and outside made my nose run. The winter chill was sniffing at Alaska's door, trying to find a way in so she could blanket the land with snow, freeze the Naknek into a rough sheet of ice, and invite long hours of darkness out to play. Already, wood smoke floated on the air.

For a moment, I considered going back inside. It still felt too soon to venture forth, to undertake an activity that wasn't required to get from one day to the next. But the thought of returning to my room, of having to answer Mom's questions about my change in plans, prompted me down the steps and out into the street.

It felt weird walking alone.

When I reached the town square, I thought maybe I'd just keep walking down some random road, skipping the game and the looks I'd no doubt receive. This would be my first social outing since the crash.

"Hey, Winter." J. C. Watson, editor at the weekly *Tundra Tribune*, waved from where he was placing more papers in the coin-operated dispenser outside the newspaper office. "Going to the game?"

"Yeah." Guess I was committed to it now.

"Hear the Homer team has a player as big as a snowplow. Hope none of our boys get hurt. I've got Chris taking notes and pictures for me." Chris, J. C.'s son, was in my class.

The image of Jesse being slammed into the boards by a snowplow made me wince.

As I walked through the town center and down Aurora Road on the other side of the square, thoughts of Jesse accompanied me. Could I say he was a friend now? He'd certainly held up his end of what friendship was supposed to be.

But did friends have the types of dreams about each other that I'd had that night about Jesse? My skin warmed at the mere thought. I shook my head, hoping to dislodge the memory. The warmth zinged through me, and my lips tingled.

I reached the rink, an oddity for rural Alaska. If it weren't for Tom Rutledge, the wealthy owner of the Brown Bear Lodge a couple of miles up the river, we wouldn't have one. He'd made his fortune in Montana real estate before cashing out and heading to Alaska. He was a huge hockey fan and had built the rink for Tundra and nearby Jasperton, even helping teams afford to fly in for games.

As I stared at the testament to his love of the game, I considered turning around and going home or heading to the river—anywhere but here.

I sat beside Spencer's bed, checking his fever by placing my palm against his forehead.

"Hey," he croaked when he saw me.

"You do know April is a really dumb month to get the flu, right?"

"I don't like to be ordinary."

I rolled my eyes and poured him a glass of water.

"How long have you been here?" he asked.

"All morning. I told your mom I'd sit with you so she could go to work."

He smiled weakly. "Hey, I might get sick more often if I get a pretty, private nurse."

CHAPTER

17

By the time I decided to enter the rink and prove to myself that there was nothing—and never would be anything—between Jesse and me, more than six minutes of the first period had elapsed. The score already stood at two to zero in favor of Homer. Even before I took a seat on the top row of the stands, I spotted the snowplow on the visiting team. Good grief, he was huge. It looked like it would take three of the Tundra/Jasperton players to handle him.

I focused on the puck, wishing that little circle of hard, frozen rubber would somehow absorb all of the disturbing thoughts that plagued me. Of course, I noticed Jesse. It was impossible not to, considering how much he was on the ice. But I forced myself to watch all the other players, too, to try to guess what they might do before they did it. The game was so fast-paced that it proved difficult to keep up with everything that was going on.

Something weird had begun to happen to me by the time the first period drew to a close. I'd begun to "ohhh" when snowplow boy, whose jersey read Ooglichuk, knocked Tundra players out of the way like pesky mosquitoes. When Shawn Petterson made the first goal for Tundra, I cheered along with the rest of the parents and students in the stands. Instead of leaving as I'd originally thought I might, I wandered out to the concession stand.

Monica, whose brother Charlie was on the team, handed me my popcorn. "Can't remember seeing you at many hockey games before."

"Felt like getting out of the house, and Lindsay's on a date with Caleb."

"Those two seem to be hitting it off! I know some girls are mighty jealous."

I met her eyes as I took a sip of my drink. "You?"

"Nah. I mean, he's hot, but I met a guy online."

"Really?" I scooted out of the way of the rest of the line.

Monica leaned closer to me. "Yeah. He's from Togiak. When he sent me his picture, I almost fell out of my chair. On my honor, he's the best-looking guy I've ever seen. I'm thinking about asking if he could come here for the Snow Ball."

Evidently, Mr. Online in Togiak was hot enough to make her forget about her previous lusting over Ryan Davis.

Just when life had given me a temporary reprieve, the mention of the dance drained away any enjoyment. God, this was going to keep happening until that stupid dance was over.

"Winter?"

I didn't want Monica's concern, so I dipped my fingers into my popcorn and acted as if her words hadn't twisted my heart into painful contortions. "If he's that hot, you better be prepared to knock off girls with Charlie's hockey stick."

Monica laughed, then stepped to her left to take an order. "I'll catch you later, okay?"

I nodded and retraced my steps to my seat. Part of me wanted to leave, to distance myself from the images of Spencer. But if I was honest with myself, I'd admit they would just follow me wherever I went. So I might as well stay and see if the game could carry me away again.

The Tundra guys came out fast at the first of the second period, and Jesse scored a goal, followed by a game-tying goal by Charlie less than a minute later. That unexpected turn of events left the Homer team looking baffled. By then, the entire home crowd was rocking. The sound system blasted Guns N' Roses' "Welcome to the Jungle."

People all around the rink stood and danced, clapped, screamed.

I didn't feel like dancing, but the clapping came naturally. Why hadn't I ever enjoyed hockey games enough to come to them more often? The feeling making its way through the crowd was infectious, and I noticed it was affecting the players as well. Tundra/Jasperton's in a good way. Homer's, not so much.

I found myself sitting closer to the edge of my seat, desperately trying to keep track of where the puck was on the ice. When Jesse got slammed into the boards by two of Homer's frustrated players, I gasped and covered my mouth with my hand. How did he take that kind of pounding and not get seriously injured? I imagined seeing him wheeled out on a gurney after the game. That image made my heart squeeze, and I found myself praying silently that he would come out of this game safely.

When he pushed away from the boards, he looked up into

the crowd and his eyes locked on mine. My breath caught in my throat until he broke eye contact and skated away. What had just happened? I'd swear it'd felt like an electrical charge had arced between us.

Guilt gnawed at me. These types of feelings were wrong. So why had I come to the game knowing their possibility existed?

Because I'd thought the dream had been a fluke.

When he flew down the ice only moments later, his skates shaving the surface of the rink into a mini snowstorm when he made quick turns, I watched his every move. Despite my guilt, I had to admit I liked watching him gliding across the ice. I tried to convince myself it was no different than watching Lindsay go in for a layup during her basketball games, but deep down I knew it wasn't. Jesse wasn't my best friend, and I wasn't rooting for him because of any loyalty.

Why was I? Maybe it was some speck of school spirit, or maybe I felt like I owed him that much support after everything that had happened between us lately. And because he had been nicer to me than I probably deserved.

It was *not* because I had any feelings for him.

Whatever the reason, I had to admit I was feeling better than I had in weeks. Spencer was still there, just below the surface, but at least I didn't feel the need to curl into a fetal position and listen to Breaking Benjamin's *Phobia* album over and over. It had been one of my favorites since its release, but now the lyrics and music seemed to take on new meaning. The chorus of "Breath" was burned into my mind: "You take the breath right out of me / You left a hole where my heart should be."

I downed both the popcorn and my Coke as I watched the rest of the game, getting better at tracking the puck as the minutes ticked by.

The biggest surprise didn't come when Alex Mifflin scored a final goal to win the game with only three seconds left on the clock. No, it was when I jumped up and screamed with the rest of the crowd because it made me happy.

I considered how strange happiness felt to me now. It felt like I was indulging in something sinful, that I would pay for it later. I shoved these disturbing thoughts aside and prepared to walk home.

I spotted Jesse immediately, off to the side talking to Coach Jorgensen, and felt color rise in my face. I needed to get out of there, fast. I headed toward the exit.

"Hey, Winter."

I stopped and took a deep breath before turning. Jesse approached, carrying his skates in one hand and his stick in the other.

"You made a game."

"Yeah. I've been hearing such good things, thought I'd check it out. Congrats on the win."

"Thanks."

I shoved my hands in my jacket pockets to hide any evidence of shaking. "How you're walking upright after the beating you took, I don't know."

He laughed. "Nothing a few bags of frozen peas won't cure."

"If I'd been hit by that Ooglichuk guy, I'd need an entire truckload of frozen peas. That or several new body parts."

"I'll admit that one hurt a little."

I smirked at the understatement. "I better get home," I said, then turned to head for the exit again.

"Winter."

An odd, sizzly feeling went through me when he said my name. As long as I'd known him, I couldn't remember ever hearing him say it in the way it sounded to me now. Deep, sexy, hopeful. What was that about? "Yeah?"

"Listen, my stepmom's having a birthday party for me next weekend. It's kind of lame, but it's something she's done for me ever since she married my dad. And Dad would rip off my head if I told her I was too old for it." He shifted his weight to the other foot and spun his stick on its handle end. "I'd like you to come over . . . if you want, that is."

Well, that was a first. Other than the annual Labor Day cookout, I didn't think I'd been invited to one of Jesse's parties. Still, I shrugged. "Sure."

It was becoming obvious that I should stay away from him, at least until the strange feelings I was having dissipated. But I couldn't seem to say no.

"Great!" He smiled, and I felt the force of that smile like the sun emerging from thick, dark clouds. "I'll see you then. Well, I'll see you before then, at school. See ya." He turned and hurried toward the locker room.

I just stared at his retreating form, trying to figure out why in the world Jesse had seemed nervous. Had hell frozen over, and everyone neglected to tell me?

I slowly turned to head outside and tried to ignore the buzz of excitement coursing through me.

"My grandmother invited me to spend the summer in Anchorage," I said as Spencer, Lindsay, and I ate lunch at our usual cafeteria table.

Spencer lowered the french fry that was halfway to his mouth. "You're not going, are you?"

Something about the way he asked the question, as if he couldn't believe I'd even consider it, would have made up my mind for me if I hadn't done so already. Did he want me to stay in Tundra as much as I wanted to see him every day? After all, it might be our last summer together.

"No."

"Good."

CHAPTER

18

Though daylight was waning when I left the game, I took my time walking home. The restlessness was back, but now my time at the game and my conversation with Jesse had tossed a heap of confusion into the mix, too. Having a good time felt so foreign, as though I'd committed some moral crime. How could happiness coexist with the heartache that still often punched me?

It seemed like half the town of Tundra had attended the game. I watched as little kids re-created plays with toy hockey sticks. Laughter filled the late-afternoon air.

"Great game, huh?" Chris Watson asked as he came up next to me and walked backward several steps.

"Yeah."

He lifted his camera. "Think I got some good pictures. Gonna be a killer season." He turned in obvious excitement and hurried toward the square, no doubt straight for the newspaper office.

I stopped and let the sounds of everyone's conversations waft past me.

"Did you see the size of the Ooglichuk guy?"

"Our team hasn't looked that good in ten years."

"We're going climbing next weekend. You want to go?"

Only a few weeks ago, these same people had attended the memorial service for Spencer, hugged and offered condolences to the Isaacs family. Now it seemed like Spencer's death was becoming a distant memory for all of them. They were getting on with their lives, and I feared part of me—the same part that had forced me to eat in the days following the crash—wanted to do the same.

But how could I, when I still missed him so much? I couldn't go to Jesse's party, even if part of me wanted very much to move on like everyone else.

As I stepped onto the square, I noticed that the lights were on in Tundra Books. I considered going over there and even took a few steps that way as I tried to figure out what I'd say to Mr. and Mrs. Isaacs. Then I faltered. I bit my bottom lip and hugged myself.

I couldn't do it. I still wasn't strong enough. Instead, I changed direction and headed down the street toward home.

When my house came into view, I noticed Lindsay sitting on the front steps. "Hey," I said as I approached within a few yards.

"Hey, yourself. I hear you went to the hockey game. That's, uh, new."

I stood on the smooth stones of the front walk and shoved my hands in my jacket pockets. "I needed something different to do."

"And hockey won the lottery."

I hesitated for a moment before answering. "Jesse invited me a few weeks back, but I didn't feel like going then."

She crossed her arms atop her knees. "It's good that you feel like going now, right?"

I shrugged. "I don't know. Maybe. Felt . . . weird. I mean, I sort of had a good time."

Lindsay didn't respond immediately.

"Since Caleb asked me out, I've thought a lot about Spencer and what he would think of how we've acted since the crash," she said. "He wouldn't want us to mourn forever." She caught and held my gaze. "He wouldn't want you to hang on so hard."

"I can't help it. Part of me thinks he's coming back, that I just have to have enough faith."

"I wish that were true."

Sounds of cars in town filled the few seconds of silence that followed.

I shifted my gaze toward the river. "I need to walk." I took off and heard Lindsay slip off the steps and follow. We didn't speak during the short walk to the river. Once we stood at the lip of the riverbank, I stared off toward the shadowy outlines of the peaks of Katmai.

"If it had been one of us, how long do you think he would have mourned?" I asked.

"I have no idea. He loved us both in different ways, but guys are different. Doesn't mean they care any less."

I inhaled slowly and let myself imagine Spencer had found some shelter to protect himself up in those forbidding mountains—that he was just biding his time until someone found him. I imagined this, even though my practical side knew it was impossible. No one was looking for him, because he was gone.

"He'd want you to be happy, Winter. Spencer didn't have a selfish bone in his body. I can't imagine any scenario where he'd want you to become a recluse."

I knew she was right, but why was it so hard to admit it?

The Stanislowski brothers, all four of them, motored by in their small, battered fishing vessel, the *Katmai Queen*—a fancy name for a very unfancy boat—and waved at us.

As we waved back, I decided to use their appearance to change the subject. "So, how did your date go?"

Lindsay scuffed at the edge of the dirt with her old hiking boot. "Are you sure you want to talk about that?"

I looked over at her. "Yes, Linds. Just because I can't decide if I want to move on doesn't mean you can't. You don't have to hide your happiness from me. Who knows, maybe it'll rub off." I tried to smile.

Lindsay waited another couple of moments before she spoke. "It was nice. We walked down the river trail, then up Mullins Road so Caleb could take some pictures. He'd never been to Alaska in the fall, so he was fascinated by the colors on the tundra."

I tried to imagine seeing the golds and reds and the bright colors of wild blueberries and bearberries for the first time, but couldn't. Those scenes had been a part of my earliest memories—they'd always been a part of me. But I figured the scene would captivate Caleb just as the Grand Canyon or the manic rush of Los Angeles would me.

"He showed me how to use his camera and the zoom lenses. I've seen the tundra a million times, but it was like I was seeing it for the first time with him."

A pang hit me as I remembered that the thought of flying with Spencer had given me a similar feeling.

"I'm glad you had a good time. He seems like a nice guy."

"He really is." She paused and stared out across the darkening tundra on the opposite side of the river. "Honestly, he reminds me a lot of Spencer. Smart, thoughtful, a good person."

I hoped she was right, because Spencer had been the gold standard. I closed my eyes and relived the kisses we'd shared through his bedroom window.

I wondered whether Mrs. Isaacs had found the carrot cakes and whether she'd known where it had come from.

"I better get home," I said.

"Are you okay?"

I nodded, not wanting to ruin her pleasant day. "Mom will just be wondering where I am."

On the way back to the house, Lindsay told me about more of her day. My initial distrust of Caleb ebbed. Maybe he represented the turning point Lindsay's life needed.

When we reached the front steps, she climbed on her bike and flipped on the small headlight. But she didn't leave.

"Is something wrong?" I asked.

She studied me. "I know how much you loved Spencer, but he'd want you to move on. At some point, that will mean dating someone else."

I was already shaking my head before all the words were out of her mouth.

She held up a hand to stop my protest. "I'm not pushing you. Only you can decide when you're ready. I just want you to know it's okay." She glanced toward the Kerrs' house. "No matter who it ends up being."

Glad the encroaching darkness hid the flush of my face, I couldn't respond. I didn't know if I could without spilling everything about Jesse, including the dream. And I didn't know if I was ready to do that until I began to understand the conflicted feelings that had begun roiling within me.

"I'll call you tomorrow," Lindsay said as she started pedaling, and waved over her shoulder.

After she was gone, I sank onto the front steps and watched the shadows stealing more of the daylight each moment.

"Spencer, what am I supposed to do?" I whispered.

"Ah, summer!" Spencer said as we exited the school on the last day of our junior year, emerging outside as seniors.

"Our last one," Lindsay said.

The last summer the three of us might spend together. That thought dampened my mood. I had only three months to decide if I'd tell Spencer how I felt about him, or if we'd go our separate ways in the fall with him none the wiser. At least we'd still be good friends. But what if I chanced telling him that I loved him as more, and he didn't feel the same? Could I take the chance of ruining our friendship forever?

"Don't look so sad," Spencer said as he draped his arm around my shoulders. "We're going to make this the best summer ever."

CHAPTER
19

I sat on a stool behind the Oregano's front counter, doodling geometric shapes on the back of my order pad. Casey had run to the bank to make a quick deposit, and Lindsay wasn't due out of basketball practice for another thirty minutes. In the meantime, I'd managed to put together the one pizza order that had come in.

During my non-busy moments, I thought of Jesse. I'd waffled back and forth on whether to go to his party since he'd invited me two nights before. My answer changed with each mood swing. Today was a bit of an up day, so I was leaning toward going. As strange as it seemed, all the signs I was getting from him indicated he liked me. Liked me, as in a *potential-girlfriend* kind of way. Bookish girl and hot hockey player—in what world besides fiction did that kind of pairing happen?

I found myself wondering about him, what he was really like. Not what I'd assumed over the past few years. What did he want to do with his life? Did he aspire to leaving Alaska, as Spencer had? As I did? I had no idea if he was good enough to play in the NHL; but if so, was that what he wanted? Or did he just want to stay in Tundra and take over his family's grocery business?

And what were his thoughts about me?

I kept wondering why his invitation—and the simple fact that he'd noticed me at the hockey game—made me feel strange. Maybe it was to be expected when people from two circles collided. We didn't know how to speak each other's languages, necessarily, but were fascinated by each other nonetheless.

I'd started doodling a "J" on the pad when the front door opened. I looked up to see Mrs. Isaacs walking toward me, her steps hesitant. Guilt that I hadn't gone to see her—that I'd been thinking of another guy instead of Spencer—clawed at me from the inside. Her appearance felt like a smack on my face. One I deserved.

She gave me a small smile.

"Hi, Winter."

My voice broke when I tried to speak. I had to swallow before trying again. "Hi." We stared at each other for several awkward seconds, and that made me sad. Shame threatened to steal my breath. "Can . . . can I get you something?"

She looked at the menu above my head, as though she'd never stepped foot in Oregano's. "I think I'd like an Italian sub."

I scratched out the "J" with more pressure than necessary and flipped over the pad to write down her order. I handed it to Casey as she came in and hurried by me to the kitchen.

Spencer's mom lifted a hand, and I noticed she held a

Tundra Books bag. "The book you had on back order came in. I'm sorry. I've had it more than a week. I . . . I think I was trying to build up the courage to bring it over."

The lump in my throat swelled to baseball size, and I fought tears when I accepted the bag, which was like so many others I'd accepted from Spencer over the years. I didn't want to cry in front of Mrs. Isaacs, but it was difficult to hold it together. How clearly I remembered the last time I'd asked him about this book—a costume-design manual I'd coveted.

"Is that book ever going to get here?" I'd asked him in frustration.

Spencer had leaned across the counter and smiled at me. "When it arrives, I'll bring it to you personally. We aim to please at Tundra Books."

Sadness washed over me that he hadn't been able to keep his promise. Guilt followed the sadness as I realized that a more-than-friendly interest was building between Jesse and me, despite how I still felt about Spencer.

I refocused on the fact that Mrs. Isaacs was standing in front of me. I'd deal with my own problems later.

"I'm sorry I haven't been to the store," I said, unable to meet her eyes.

She placed her hand atop mine on the counter. "I understand. We both needed time."

I looked at her and noticed how much older she looked than she had only two months ago. I'd lost a great friend, someone I'd loved, but how horrible must it be to lose an only child? I couldn't imagine how she and Mr. Isaacs even got out of bed in the morning. There were days when I didn't think I would be able to expend that much energy.

She squeezed my hand with gentle pressure. "I wanted to thank you for always being such a wonderful friend to Spencer. And I'm sorry you didn't get the chance to be more."

God, my heart nearly split at the thought that Spencer had told his mother about his feelings.

All I could do without breaking down was nod as she squeezed my hand and accepted her sandwich. Then she was gone.

Casey placed her hand on my back. "Do you need a break?"

I shook my head. I knew if I started crying, I wouldn't stop. "I'll be fine in a minute." Or a year, or maybe never.

As if fate hadn't heaped enough on me, a little while after Spencer's mom left, Jesse and some of his hockey team-mates came in, their faces still flushed from practice. That scratched-out "J" on the back of the order pad taunted me. What had I been thinking?

I swallowed the fresh sorrow and forced myself to their table. Thankfully, Drew wasn't with them, so at least I didn't have to deal with him. My body felt like it was going to shake into jagged shards from the effort of holding in the urge to cry. God, I was so tired of crying.

"What can I get you all?"

"Large pepperoni, large supreme, and a pitcher of Coke," Charlie said.

"And toss in some garlic bread sticks," Jesse added.

I made the mistake of looking at him. His dark eyes showed an affection for me that was hard to accept. So I broke eye contact and turned away as I was still writing the final part of the order.

I handed the ticket to Casey, then went to the drink fountain for the Coke. I heard footsteps approaching, but I ignored them. I was so afraid they were his.

"Hey, you okay?"

"Mmm-hmm." I kept my gaze focused on the steady stream of Coke as it filled the pitcher.

He took a couple more steps and leaned on the counter in front of me. "No, you're not. What's wrong?"

I tried to wave off his concern. "Nothing." When I slid the pitcher across the counter to him, he caught my hand. He held it tightly, forcing me to meet his eyes.

Unable to hold it in any longer, I let out a slow, shaky breath. "I just talked to Spencer's mom . . . for the first time since his funeral. It brought up a lot of the pain again."

I wasn't about to spill how I'd been thinking about his party and how I'd felt guilty about it the moment I saw Mrs. Isaacs. Or how much I'd really loved Spencer—still did. How I missed him as if some part of myself had been ripped away.

Or how he, Jesse, was making me feel things I didn't think I had a right to feel.

As if sensing those feelings, he ran his thumb across the back of my hand. A warm, tingling sensation fanned out from where he touched me, swiftly spreading throughout the rest of my body.

"I hope it gets better soon."

I met his gaze and realized that his words held a double meaning. While he might genuinely hope I'd get over my grief, I got the feeling he was waiting for some sign that he could make a bigger move.

Was I dreaming again? Because this scenario couldn't be real.

"Come on, Jess, I'm thirsty," Alex Mifflin called out from the table.

Jesse hesitated before letting go of my hand, and he held my gaze a few beats longer.

"Things happen when we least expect them," he said. "But I think they happen for a reason."

I found myself nodding, agreeing with his logic even though somewhere deep down I realized it meant that Spencer's death had happened for a reason other than stripping him of his chance for a long, happy life.

Jesse reached forward and caressed my hand again. "If you want to talk later, when you get home, call me."

A new emotion—gratefulness—bloomed, joining the others that were doing a turbulent dance inside me. I was touched by the sincerity of his offer and couldn't believe this was the same Jesse Kerr I'd gone to school with since the sixth grade.

Accompanying the gratefulness, however, were nerves. Lots of them. I could tell by the look in his eyes that he'd like to do more than just talk.

And I was surprised by how much I was tempted to take him up on his offer.

"I bet you won't be able to see the stars like this in L.A.," Spencer said as he lay beside me in my backyard, staring up at the constellations blanketing the sky.

"No, I'll see stars of the movie variety."

"Maybe I'll fly down, and you can show me all the homes of the stars."

"And maybe, if you're really nice, I'll come home on occasion and we can watch the sky."

"Then I'll be really, really nice."

The way he said it, deeper and slower than usual, made a delicious chill race across my skin.

CHAPTER

20

By the time I left Oregano's, my common sense had begun to return. The idea of talking to Jesse—especially about Spencer—while knowing how Jesse seemed to feel about me was just too weird. Even if he wasn't the least bit interested romantically—and the possibility that he was seemed surreal—what good would talking about my lingering sorrow do anyway? After all, discussing it with Lindsay had been difficult enough!

Mom and Dad told me that the only thing that was going to help was time. Maybe they were right, but I couldn't imagine enough time passing that would erase my feelings for Spencer and my sense of loss.

I could have gone home with Lindsay, but I didn't want my mood to bring her down. Mom and Dad had flown to a medical conference in Anchorage that morning, so tonight I'd have to stay home alone. It didn't scare me. I mean, we weren't in a crime-ridden city or anything. But being alone with my thoughts tonight made me want to be anywhere but my own mind. I was afraid the sorrow might fill up all the empty space in the house. That, or I'd have way too much time to consider the unexpected temptation that came in the form of the boy next door.

I didn't notice anyone else on the street as I approached the house, not until Jesse spoke.

"Hey."

I jumped, then immediately felt like an idiot. Though darkness lay heavy on Tundra, I could see him standing at his family's mailbox, several envelopes in hand. His house shed just enough light to reveal his shape.

My face heated, and I wondered if he could see me glowing in the dark.

Just act normal.

"Hey. Little late to be getting the mail, isn't it?"

"Yeah. Brenda forgot," he said.

I wondered if I should go inside. I was having to fight way too hard to resist thinking about him in a way I'd only ever thought about Spencer.

"She just made some brownies. They're still hot," he said. "Want some?"

I hesitated, but the lure of brownies and human interaction versus the loneliness of my house was too much to resist. "Okay."

Once we entered the Kerrs' house, Jesse led the way toward the kitchen, though I could have just as easily followed the comforting smell of fresh-baked brownies that lingered in the air.

"Well, hi, Winter," Brenda said from behind the kitchen counter. "Nice to see you."

"Thanks. You too." What an odd conversation. We saw

each other all the time. You couldn't live in Tundra, right next door to someone, and not see each other.

Jesse tossed a few brownies onto a plate before taking my hand. "Come on."

I didn't resist as he guided me toward the back porch. I felt oddly powerless to make any sort of objection. I didn't want to, even though guilt burned inside me.

The porch's screened windows were always open in the warmer months, allowing the Kerrs to sit outside and not be eaten alive by Alaska's insatiable mosquitoes. But now the windows were all shut against the damp, chilly October air. Frost formed around the exterior edges.

Jesse released my hand as he placed the plate of brownies on a small, wooden table between two white Adirondack chairs similar to the ones on our back deck.

We sat in silence, chewing on our respective brownies for a couple of minutes, before the silence got to me. "These are amazing," I said. "Just what I needed."

He glanced over at me, and I noticed he'd let his long hair grow even more. The dark brown waves brushed his collar. It suited him, and I had to admit it was übersexy.

"Thought you could use some chocolate. And I like the company." There it was again, a deeper meaning to words that were just friendly on the surface.

More silence stretched between us, and I struggled with my response. Flustered, I took a too-big bite of brownie and turned away so I could chew and swallow without him seeing how nervous he was making me.

Jeez, I felt like I was in Bizarro Tundra, where nothing

made sense. Maybe when I'd slammed into him on Labor Day, I'd slipped into an alternate universe where Spencer was gone and Jesse Kerr was attracted to me instead of girls like Patrice Murray.

Even Patrice was crazy.

More details about the cause of the fight had leaked out and been whispered around school. Word was that Jesse wasn't enough for Patrice, and she'd been seeing someone else behind his back. The gossip chain hadn't revealed who guy No. 2 was yet, but it was only a matter of time. Secrets didn't stay secrets in Tundra.

What was wrong with Patrice? Sure, I'd been in love with Spencer for years, but I wasn't so blind that I couldn't appreciate Jesse's good looks. He was tall with longish dark-chestnut hair and eyes barely a shade lighter. And as I was figuring out, he was a decent guy. So unless Patrice had Paul Walker or Vin Diesel waiting in a hidden cabin somewhere, she was stupid.

"Are you doing better than earlier?" he asked.

I thought a moment, then nodded. "I feel like I'm riding a yo-yo sometimes. Up one minute, down the next."

He didn't respond immediately, so I looked in his direction. Something about the tight expression on his face made me wonder if he didn't really want to talk about what I felt for Spencer. God, as impossible as it seemed, was I hurting him?

He met my eyes. "I know what it's like to lose someone."

I hadn't expected that response. "Patrice?"

He laughed bitterly. "No." Moments passed as he took another bite of brownie, chewed, swallowed. "My mom left when I was eight, just disappeared. We thought something horrible had happened, until a month later when we got a letter from Colorado saying she just didn't want to be a wife or mother anymore."

It took a moment for the shock of his revelation to sink in. "That's horrible."

"Yeah, pretty much sucked."

Everyone knew his dad was divorced, and none of us had ever seen Jesse's mom, but this had never entered my mind as a possibility.

"Have you heard from her since then?"

Jesse shook his head as he grabbed yet another brownie. Looked like I wasn't the only one who needed a chocolate fix.

"Don't really want to, either. I did at first because I missed her. Then I wanted to see her so I could tell her what a pathetic mother she was. Then I just stopped caring."

I tried to imagine a child version of Jesse looking out the window of his bedroom, wondering when his mother was going to come home. Only she never did. My heart squeezed for that little boy.

"Things got better when Dad met Brenda a couple of years later, then bought the store down here and we moved. She's always tried so hard to make me feel wanted, you know?" He glanced over his shoulder to see if Brenda was within earshot. "That's why I go along with the pizza and games party each year."

"It's really sweet of her. Plus, what else are we going to do? Tundra isn't exactly a hotbed of nightspots."

"True. And this'll be the last one."

Next year at this time, Tundra would be in our past. Some would stay, but many of us were bound for other places. Anchorage, Fairbanks, Seattle, other points outside. I no longer knew where my own path would take me, but I doubted my parents would let me hide in my room the rest of my life.

"Does anyone else know?"

"Nope. You're the first."

"Why tell me?"

Our eyes met, and I experienced the oddest sensation that I could fall in and drown in those dark depths.

"I like you." He paused for the briefest moment. "And you're easy to talk to. More real than most people."

I shifted my gaze to the windows, the clear night outside. If we shut off the house lights, we'd probably be able to see the stars. I heard a sigh from Jesse, one that sounded both frustrated and resigned.

"Spencer was a good guy," Jesse said, abruptly changing topics. "I liked him."

"He was the best." I paused for a moment. "We were supposed to have our first date that night, to celebrate him getting his pilot's license."

Like Jesse, I'd shared something deep and personal. Something about the half dark, the shared sense of loss, the odd comfort made it easy to talk to him despite our unspoken feelings.

"You'd liked him a long time, hadn't you?"

I hesitated, considered how sharing further information about Spencer might affect Jesse. I still could only half believe his feelings for me were a possibility. Finally, I decided on honesty.

"Since elementary school. I only got up the nerve to say something a few days before. . . ."

I left out the kissing and other intimate details, but otherwise he got the whole story of how I'd liked Spencer since second grade. I should have stopped right there, but it was as if my mouth were a runaway train.

"We'd planned to go to the Snow Ball," I said. "I was so excited. Doesn't seem important now."

Jesse leaned forward, angling himself closer to me. "Maybe you'll still go."

I held my breath for a moment, afraid he might ask me. And afraid of what I might say in response.

"So what's in the bag?" Jesse gestured toward my Tundra Books bag.

For a heartbeat, I hesitated before pulling out *Dressed: A Century of Hollywood Costume Design* and showing him the cover.

"It's written by a designer who's been nominated for an Academy Award." I allowed myself to indulge in a brief glimpse of my own Oscar fantasy. "I used to think I wanted to be a costume designer."

"You don't now?"

I returned the pristine book to the bag, wondering if I'd ever take it out again. "I don't know anymore. I haven't drawn since before the crash." I sighed. "Feels like that part of me died, too."

"Maybe it's just hibernating."

I looked at his profile and realized Jesse was smarter and more mature than I'd ever given him credit for. "Waiting for spring, metaphorically speaking?"

"When you lose someone, lots of things go on hold. But you eventually come out of the fog and want to live again. New things replace what you lost."

But no one could replace Spencer. It was cruel to let Jesse think he could, if indeed that was where his thoughts were leading him. How could I say that, though, when I wasn't even sure of my perceptions? What if I was totally off base and made an enormous fool of myself?

"That sounds like it came from a self-help book," I said with a hint of a laugh, trying to lighten the mood.

He shrugged. "For all I know, it did. It's probably something I remembered from the counselor Dad made me see after Mom left."

I could tell he was spinning a story. Not that he hadn't seen a counselor, but that his words had been repeated from some long-ago session. He'd shared something profound with me, and I'd made light of it. I felt terrible.

Jesse pointed at the Tundra Books bag. "For what it's worth, I think it's cool. You should go for it."

I picked at a stray thread sticking out from the side seam of my jeans. "It's hard to imagine going that far away, leaving Alaska and everyone behind."

"Why can't you draw your designs here?"

"The school I'd planned to go to is in California. And if I wanted to work in the movie industry, Hollywood isn't moving to Anchorage anytime soon."

I thought I saw a flicker of sadness in Jesse's eyes—another sign that this night had to exist in some alternate dimension.

"Well, Alaska isn't going anywhere. You can always come back and visit."

The strangest thought entered my head, that Jesse would be among the people I'd miss if I ever left Tundra behind.

"What about you? What are your plans?" I really wanted to know.

"File that under 'I Don't Know,' too. Everyone probably expects me to take over the store when Dad retires."

"Doesn't sound too exciting."

He laughed. "What? You don't think a rewarding career in the grocery business is exciting?"

He said it with such a straight face that I laughed, too. I realized how little I'd laughed in recent weeks. It felt weird, and yet good at the same time. Yet another thing I should thank him for.

I still felt the tug of a smile on my lips a few minutes later, when I noticed how much time had passed. "I'd better get home. Thanks for the brownies." I eyed the nearly empty plate. "I think I need to run to King Salmon and back to work off the calories."

When I started to stand, Jesse jumped to his feet and extended his hand to help me up. I wavered for a moment before placing mine in his. It was just a helpful gesture, I told myself.

He pulled me to my feet, but he didn't let go once I was standing before him, closer than I expected. His lips parted. "Winter."

I leaned forward before something clicked in my brain—common sense—and I stepped backward.

I made myself smile, but I couldn't quite meet his eyes. "Thanks again. I'll see you at school."

I wanted to say more, to thank him for everything: for listening, for sharing his own story, and even for the feelings he hadn't spoken, because even though they scared me, they also helped make me feel alive. I hoped Spencer would forgive me for my weakness.

Jesse didn't follow me as I stepped back out into the chilly night. I took a few seconds to breathe deeply of the crisp air before heading for my empty house.

The almost kiss was still zipping through my brain when I rounded the fence. I could barely distinguish someone sitting on the top of my front steps. I froze and sucked in a breath, considering retreat. But then the figure looked my way, and I realized it was Lindsay. What was she doing here this late? Oregano's had closed an hour before.

Lindsay startled me by jumping up and running toward me. When she wrapped me in her arms, I heard her sniffles.

"I thought something had happened to you," she said.

"No, I'm fine. Sorry, I didn't know you were coming over."

Lindsay's continued crying worried me because, despite everything she'd been through, Linds didn't often cry. She typically got mad and threw things or cursed. I pulled back and looked at her face, then sucked in another breath. Jesse's house shed just enough illumination to reveal the bruise marring her left cheek.

"I love it, Linds," I said as I pulled the red-and-white knit scarf from the package.

"You better. It took me six months to make the thing."

I leaned over and kissed her on the cheek. "Thank you."

"Sorry, I didn't knit you a sweater," Spencer said.

I laughed. "Good. I'd hate to see what that would look like."

He handed me a package. When I ripped away the wrapping and opened the box inside, I found a Quote-a-Day calendar and a certificate from the International Star Registry. I read the text on the certificate and felt myself tearing up. I met Spencer's eyes and, unbelievably, fell more in love with him in that instant.

"You named a star after me?"

"It seemed appropriate."

CHAPTER 21

"*Oh* my God, Linds," I said as I turned her more fully toward the light and examined the damage. "Did Caleb do this to you?"

She pulled away. "No!" She sounded horrified that I'd think so. "It was Dad."

The fact that she hadn't called him "the sperm donor" told me how upset she really was. "I thought he left."

"He came back, obviously." She shivered, so I wrapped my arm around her shoulders and guided her inside the warmth of my house.

"Was he drunk?" Even so, Lindsay had said he'd always focused his rage on her mom, not her or her brothers.

"When is he *not* drunk?"

I steered her to the kitchen, where I retrieved a bag of frozen corn, wrapping it in a thin dish towel and pressing it gently to her face.

"What happened?"

"He came back stinking pissed, ran the truck right over Seth's bike, then had the nerve to stomp in yelling about how it'd been in his way." She slammed the side of her fist against the top of the kitchen table. "The bike was a good ten feet off the driveway. Of course, he was too far gone to realize that he'd missed the driveway entirely."

She let out a shaky breath that caught on an angry sob she managed to wrangle into submission.

"I'd had it, Winter." She choked on another sob before shaking it off, too. "I told him exactly what a pathetic loser I thought he was and that we'd all be better off if someone tossed him in the middle of the Bering Sea."

My own anger fired. "And he hit you?"

"Yep. I'm following in Mom's footsteps. What a proud moment."

I wrapped my hands around her fist, shook it until she looked at me. "You're not like her, Linds. You stood up to him, and then you left."

A tear escaped her eye and ran down the cheek that hadn't been damaged by her dad's ham of a hand. I wiped it away, then pulled her into my arms. "I know you don't like to show weakness, but crying isn't weakness. Sometimes it's the healthiest thing you can do."

My words must have picked away the final piece of mortar holding her dam together. It broke, and all her hurt and anger and disillusionment came pouring out onto my shoulder. I held her and let her cry until she couldn't anymore.

When I pulled back so she could wipe her nose, I ran my hand over her hair. "Where's Seth?"

"Spending the night at Heath Corgin's, thank God."

I waited until her eyes met mine. "We need to call the police. This can't happen again."

A shadow passed over her eyes, and I knew she was dreading the additional embarrassment this would cause her when word got out. Still, she nodded bravely.

I made the call to the police department, and within five minutes, Chief Elachik, a round-chested Yupik man roughly the size of a fishing trawler, showed up. Chief's sheer size was enough to keep most of Tundra on the right side of the law. I watched his dark complexion redden as Lindsay related the entire story to him.

"I'm sure he's long gone by now," Lindsay said, sounding half defeated and half relieved.

Chief patted her knee. "Don't you worry about that. I'm pretty good at finding folks don't want to be found."

And I'd hate to be Lindsay's dad when he did. Chief looked like he might revert to drawing and quartering as a suitable punishment.

When I let Chief Elachik out the door, Jesse had been standing outside, about to knock.

"Are you okay?" Jesse asked as he looked back at me, worry etching every line of his face. It tugged at what remained of my heart.

"Yes, fine."

"Why was the chief here?"

Aware of Lindsay in the room behind me, I replied in a low voice. "I can't really say."

Jesse's brows bunched. "You're sure you're okay? Do you need anything?" He glanced inside, but I wasn't sure if the angle would reveal Lindsay's presence.

"I'm fine, really. Go on back. It's nearly eleven o'clock."

He glanced behind me again. "Call if you need anything."

I nodded and shut the door quickly when he turned before he decided to ask something else.

Of course, then I had to face the questions written on Lindsay's face. "Does that happen often?"

I pushed away from the door. "No. But then Chief isn't at my house in the middle of the night too often."

"He sounded really concerned."

"Linds, now isn't the time to discuss this."

"Of course it is. I'm sick to death of talking about this." She pointed at her blooming bruise. "My a-hole of a father doesn't deserve any more of my time. I'd much rather talk about why Jesse Kerr was at your door in the middle of the night."

"I saw him and his mom earlier. They know Mom and Dad aren't home."

"Yet it was Jesse, not his parents, who came over to check on you."

I knew she was trying to take her mind off her own problems by focusing on me and this latest development. Still, it made me squirm as I sat in the cushy living room chair. I pulled a plush throw over my legs, preparing for the inevitable conversation.

"What's going on?"

"Nothing," I said, the words feeling like a lie on my tongue. "Not yet anyway."

Lindsay's eyes widened, like I'd just told her I was part of the Witness Protection Program. "I knew there was something there."

I shook my head. "I just hung out with him some tonight. Talked." I picked at a torn cuticle, absurdly nervous at the idea of telling Lindsay everything. "He was in Oregano's earlier when I was upset because Spencer's mom came in. He invited me over. I didn't think I'd go at first, but . . ." I looked at the stairs that led to my bedroom. "I couldn't face an empty house. So I caved and went over there."

"What did you two do?"

"Just ate some brownies and talked about Spencer, Patrice, stuff." I looked at her, wishing we'd found another topic to get her mind off her craptacular home life.

"What are you not telling me?"

Still, I hesitated. "I think he almost kissed me." I wrung my hands. "I'm getting all these signals from him that don't make any sense. Even thinking that Jesse could like me is laughable."

"Why?" Linds sounded genuinely confused.

"Because we're nothing alike." Which wasn't exactly true, was it?

"Do you like him?"

"I don't know. I mean, he's nicer than I gave him credit for." She'd understand more if I told her about his mom, but that wasn't my secret to tell. And some lonely part of me felt special that I was the only one in whom he'd confided.

"Winter, I know you're still hurting over Spencer. Sometimes I still cry when I think about him, too. But maybe it's time to take another step forward. If you like Jesse, consider acting on it while he's still single. I'm surprised he still is, to be honest."

I thought about what he'd told me about his mom's aban-
donment, then the rumors I'd heard about Patrice's secret
guy. Maybe Jesse was a little gun-shy about starting another
relationship, and I couldn't blame him.

"I don't know if I can."

"Just think about it."

Lindsay's question burrowed its way into my brain, and
I didn't know how to answer it. Did I like Jesse? Yes. Did I
like like him? I thought I did, but I didn't know whether to
trust my feelings.

Neither of us could settle down enough to sleep, so I
made us hot chocolate and we sank side by side onto the
couch to watch *Pride and Prejudice*, the Keira Knightley–
Matthew MacFadyen version. For a little while we set aside
real-life questions, family problems, and boys and allowed
ourselves to drool over Mr. Darcy. He made it so easy.

Lindsay snuggled farther under the blanket. "I can't wait
until you're working on some movie like this, and I can utilize
my best-friend privileges and get to hang out on the set."

I didn't respond, just kept my eyes focused on the dance
scene. The costumes *were* beautiful, weren't they?

"You still haven't drawn, have you?" she asked, clasping my
hand over the blanket. "Don't keep your life on hold forever."

When I didn't respond, she turned her attention to the
movie.

We'd fallen so far into the story that we both yelped
when someone knocked on the front door. I glanced at the
clock—it was now closing in on 12:30. The idea that it might
be Lindsay's dad entered my mind and chilled my blood.

I grabbed the cordless phone and gave it to Lindsay. "Stay out of sight. If you hear your dad's voice, call Chief Elachik."

"I doubt it's him. That would take too much effort."

"Just in case. Who else is going to show up after midnight?"

"Maybe it's Jesse again." There was a note of teasing in her voice—remarkable, after what she'd been through tonight. But also very Lindsay.

I gave her a narrow-eyed "cut it out" look, then eased my way to the door. I held my breath as I peeked out the little window that was cut into the thick wood of the door. Caleb Moore stood on the porch, wearing a parka and looking as if he were freezing. Silly outsider—his blood hadn't thickened enough yet to deal with Alaska's temperatures.

I shot my attention back to Lindsay and whispered, "It's Caleb."

"What!" She leaped off the couch and poised to make a run for the back door. "Don't open it."

"I have to open it. If we don't come to the door, he might think something's wrong and call for help." Though if he was turning blue on my front porch this late, chances were he'd snuck out.

"How did he know I was here? Oh God, what if he knows what happened?"

"He's the mayor's stepson, so he probably does. You knew this wouldn't stay secret, but we'll deal with it. And it's just common sense that you'd come here if you didn't feel safe at home."

Lindsay hugged herself, making her look half her age.

When I unlocked the door, I heard her hurry down the hall and into the bathroom.

"Caleb, what are you doing here?" I asked when I opened the door.

"Is Lindsay all right?"

"She's fine. Go on home before you freeze to death."

"I want to see her."

"I don't think—"

"Please."

There was so much need and yearning in his voice— so much worry darkening his blue eyes—that I caved and opened the door. As he stepped inside, I heard Lindsay squeak down the hall, then the bathroom door shutting and locking.

"She doesn't want you to see her like this," I said low, hoping Linds wouldn't hear me. "She's embarrassed."

"She doesn't have to be embarrassed with me."

I motioned toward the bathroom. "Tell her that."

He took off his gloves and shoved them in his parka pockets as he headed down the hall. I wandered into the kitchen, nibbling on some Cheez-Its as I listened to Caleb try to convince Lindsay to come out of the bathroom.

"No," she said. "I look wretched."

"I doubt that, and anyway, it wouldn't matter."

"It *does* matter." I heard the strangled sob in her voice and knew she'd hate herself later for allowing him to hear it. "You don't understand what it's like, how embarrassing it is."

The silence hung so long that I wondered if he'd given up. If he did, would that hurt Lindsay, even though she'd told him to go away?

I peeked around the wall of the kitchen and saw Caleb still outside the door, his palm flattened against it.

"It doesn't matter to me what kind of man your father is. I like *you*."

"I like you, too. That's why I don't want you to see me like this."

He sighed. "Lindsay, I know what it's like, to be ashamed of a family member. My mom divorced my dad because he was having an affair with my fifth-grade teacher."

God, was there anyone our age who didn't have some tale of woe? Someone who hadn't disappointed them in a scarring way?

The silence hung heavy in the hallway, and my heart ached for both Lindsay and Caleb. All the doubts I'd ever had about him had faded away. She was right. His caring and tenderness reminded me of Spencer and the way he'd treated me. My vision blurred, and I had to blink away the tears that the realization encouraged.

I watched as Lindsay cracked the door, then opened it wider and walked into Caleb's arms. He held her close, rubbing his hand over her long, black hair and whispering reassurances. Unable to watch the tenderness, I went up to my room.

From the window, I stared at the moon shining on the snow atop the distant mountains, covering the spot where Spencer had lost his life. I placed my hand against the cold pane, as if his memory was tangible and I could feel its warmth. That wishful part of me imagined him hiking through those fierce mountains toward home.

I knew those imaginings were just prolonging my grief, but I couldn't fully let them go. Still . . .

My gaze lowered and fixed on the Kerrs' house. I wondered if Lindsay could be right—if Jesse could maybe turn into something more than just the boy next door.

"Love makes your soul crawl out from its hiding place."
—Zora Neale Hurston, *Quote-a-Day* calendar

CHAPTER

22

Despite her long talk with Caleb the night before, Lindsay balked when I woke her for school.

"I don't want to go. Everyone is going to know all the gory details already." She massaged her forehead with the tips of her fingers as if she had a headache just thinking about it. "Sometimes this town nearly smothers me."

I understood about the suffocation. The past two months, it'd felt as if everyone I saw was watching me to see if I'd crack. I imagined them taking bets down at the Blue Walrus and wondered what the odds were running.

There wasn't an ounce of doubt that local tongues had been wagging since I'd placed the call to Chief Elachik last night, and the chatter about Dimitri's latest transgression wasn't going away anytime soon.

"You know, it won't be any better tomorrow or the next day, so you might as well get it over with."

"It might, if I wait until the bruise is gone." She gently touched her cheek.

Anger on her behalf made me want to hunt down her dad myself and smack him hard with whatever was handy.

"No, the longer you stay away, the worse it'll get. You know this."

Lindsay flopped back on the couch. "I'm tired."

"What time did Caleb leave?"

"Around three."

"He braved sneaking out and nearly froze his Lower 48 ass to come see you. You can brave the gossip of people with nothing better to do."

She groaned but dragged herself off the couch and toward the bathroom. By the time we both were ready to leave, we opened the door to find Caleb on the front steps, ready to be Lindsay's buffer. And because he had his own truck, we got a warm ride to school instead of a chilly walk.

Flanked by both of us, Lindsay seemed to regain some of her self-confidence. When we reached Caleb's locker, he gave her a kiss on her bruised cheek. I stuck close to Lindsay's side as we made our way down the hall to our lockers. We acted as if nothing was out of the ordinary, even though I caught occasional glances and whispers. When we reached our lockers, it felt as if we'd successfully run a gauntlet.

I saw Patrice walking toward us with her minion, Skyler Thornby. I couldn't get to Lindsay before Patrice, to drag her away from whatever Patrice was up to. Ever since the day she'd given me the narrow-eyed look in the hallway when I'd been talking to Jesse, I'd been avoiding her as much as possible.

But as I prepared to jump to Lindsay's defense, Patrice walked by, giving Lindsay's arm a gentle squeeze. Lindsay looked surprised. It was only a moment, however, before

Patrice gave me the same ugly look she usually kept under wraps. It had definitely never been seen by adults. How she'd kept the not-so-nice part of herself hidden in Tundra, I'd never figure out. Maybe she'd made a deal with the devil.

"What?" I asked, more aggressively than I'd intended. I was tired of her.

She glanced around the hallway before taking a step closer and narrowing her eyes. But she didn't speak in a low voice as I'd expected. "You think you're suddenly something since Jesse noticed you, don't you?"

Shock slammed into me. What did she know? How did she know it? How could she have even expected?

Damn, this was Tundra. Why did I even ask those questions?

"We're just friends." I ignored the tug inside me that insisted we could be more if I only let it happen.

"Good. Because when I decide I want him back, I'll be able to get him like this." Patrice snapped her fingers in front of my face. I resisted the violent temptation to grab them and bend them backward until she begged for mercy. For taunting me. And for betraying Jesse. Patrice was used to getting whatever and whomever she wanted and enjoying the kudos of parents and teachers in the process. I suddenly and fervently hated her.

But what had the gesture of support to Lindsay been about? They certainly weren't in the same social circle, and that small act of kindness was so at odds with the angry queen bee in front of me.

Lindsay stepped forward, edging between Patrice and

me. Despite the hint of kindness Patrice had shown her, I was still her best friend—she'd defend me, just as I would her.

Some new emotion flitted across Patrice's face, oddly like hurt. But she backed off and gestured for Skyler to follow her down the corridor.

"Sheesh," Lindsay said. "Someone needs to tell those two they're living in Tundra, Alaska—not Upper East Side, New York."

"I feel like—I don't know—something's going on with her."

"Yeah, she's insecure."

We retrieved our books for first period and headed to our own classes. Maybe it was my imagination, but the gossip seemed to have turned in *my* direction now. I could sew Patrice's lips together for mentioning Jesse and me in the same sentence. I didn't know how I felt about Jesse, or if I would ever act on it, so the last thing I needed was the whole school gossiping about it.

For now at least, we were friends. Nothing else, just like I'd told Patrice.

I kept telling myself that as I walked into lunch three hours later and sat with Lindsay in our spot. I tried not to feel disappointed when Jesse sat in his. What was wrong with me? I was the one who'd pulled away from him when I'd thought he might kiss me.

Did everyone filing into the cafeteria think I could forget Spencer so easily? Was he already a distant memory to them? I stared down at my hamburger, wishing things could just go back to the way they'd been the day before Labor Day. Spencer and I would be together and happy. Jesse would just be the next-door neighbor I was forced to acknowledge only when we crossed paths. Patrice would be so far off my radar I'd barely even be thinking about her.

But things couldn't go back, and I had no idea how I wanted them to go forward.

"What do you think he ever saw in Patrice?" Lindsay nodded in Jesse's direction.

I shrugged. "He's a guy, and she's beautiful. Been happening for millennia."

"I would have given him more credit than that."

I finished eating the french fry I'd shoved in my mouth. "Really?"

"Yeah. He gets big points for coming over to check on you last night."

I looked outside at the snowflakes as I replayed the previous evening. The conversation with Jesse, the near kiss, and his look of genuine concern when he'd shown up at the door. If I let go of my sorrow over Spencer, I got the feeling it'd be very easy to fall for Jesse.

When some of Lindsay's basketball team came over to discuss that night's game against Dillingham, I let my gaze drift to Jesse. Today, he was wearing a light-green shirt that complemented his dark hair and eyes. Why had I never really noticed how incredibly good-looking he was before? Was it simply because I'd only had eyes for Spencer, or was Jesse more attractive now that I knew more about who he really was?

So he'd gone out with Patrice. So what? We all made mistakes. And maybe, as much as it pained me to admit it, she had a good side that wasn't fake. I nearly gagged even contemplating it, but stranger things had happened. And I couldn't discount what I'd seen earlier that morning. Something about Patrice's kind gesture toward Lindsay nagged at me, but I couldn't pinpoint why.

Part of the conversation from their table met my ears, something about Jesse's party on Saturday. Patrice might have thought she was steering me out of the way with her little accusations, but they'd only fueled my decision to go. If for no other reason than to spite her.

I realized there was nothing worth much in the way of birthday gifts for teenage guys in Tundra, and it was too late to order something. Unless . . .

"Hey, I'll catch you all later. Got to run to the ladies'," I said to Lindsay and the other girls.

When I reached the hall, however, I walked past the restroom and found a quiet spot on the bleachers in the gym. I dialed Mom's cell number.

"Hey, honey, is something wrong?" she asked.

"No." I was surprised someone hadn't told her about Lindsay already. "I need you to pick something up for me while you're in Anchorage."

"Okay."

"Jesse invited me to his birthday party on Saturday, so I was thinking maybe a Canucks shirt." I tried to sound casual, as if deciding on my own to go to a party, and a guy's party at that, was no big deal.

Either it worked, or she was wise enough not to comment. "Got it. I'll add it to the list. See you tonight."

When I hung up, I sat in the quiet of the gym and wondered when the fact that Vancouver was Jesse's favorite hockey team had sunk into my brain. Well, it was, so maybe he'd like the present more than something I could buy at Shaggy's Trading Post.

I smiled. "Take that, Patrice!"

"Why love if losing hurts so much? We love to know that we are not alone."

—C. S. Lewis, *Quote-a-Day* calendar

CHAPTER 23

Despite my determination to go to the party a few days earlier, by Saturday, I'd started second-guessing the decision.

"If I go, it'll just add fuel to Patrice's accusations," I said as Lindsay and I ate the French toast Mom had made us. Not to mention, I couldn't shake the feeling that I should steer as far away from Jesse as possible. Something was happening, and I wasn't sure I was ready for it.

"Who gives a flying caribou turd what she thinks," she said.

My inner questioning disappeared as I snorted and choked on my syrupy bite. When I managed to swallow, I took a different approach.

"It's not really my crowd anyway, and I don't want to go without you."

"I'm working today. Plus, I'm not the one birthday boy sat with for two hours the other night."

"Do you have to keep bringing that up?"

"Yes."

For a moment, it felt like old times. But then I saw her bruised cheek and remembered the dream that had woken me that morning. In it, I'd been standing in the fog, waiting for an approaching plane to land. I'd known it was Spencer, coming back safe and sound. The plane they'd found on the mountain hadn't been his after all. But when the plane had emerged from the thick, gray, low clouds, I could see Spencer's skeleton in the pilot's seat.

I'd jerked awake only to realize that a real plane had taken off from the airstrip and was flying over our house. Luckily, Lindsay had been in the bathroom, so I didn't have to go into an explanation for my abrupt awakening.

Mom walked into the kitchen and placed a gift-wrapped box on the table next to me. "Here's the shirt. I had them gift wrap it for you." Because I am horrendous at wrapping gifts. It's like my IQ suddenly plummeted when I had to figure out how much paper a certain box would require and how best to fold it at the edges. "Oh, and I had to get a jersey, because I couldn't find a tee."

Yikes, jerseys weren't cheap. Was it too big a gift to give him? No chance to change it now.

Lindsay waited until Mom left the room again before she gave me a curious grin. "You had your mom bring him a present all the way from Anchorage?"

"What was I supposed to get him, thermals from Shaggy's?"

The present, wrapped in its dark-blue-and-yellow-striped paper, guilted me into going to the party. Lindsay hated that she had to go to work and couldn't help me get ready, but secretly I was glad. There was no way I was going to dress up and primp in hopes that Jesse Kerr would notice. Especially not when that morning's dream still lingered in my room like a ghost, shaming me.

But that dream also helped me make the decision to go. I needed to get out of the house, forget. So after pulling on jeans and a red turtleneck and pulling my hair into a low ponytail, I headed next door.

My procrastinating meant the party was already in full swing when I arrived. I placed the present on the table with the rest, then wandered through the crowd. Everyone was playing Guitar Hero on the big screen, eating nachos, and sitting around talking in groups.

"Hey," Monica said as she popped in from the garage. "Want something to drink?"

"Sure." I followed Monica into the kitchen. I grabbed a Coke and one of the now-familiar brownies.

"Come on," Monica said. "Jesse's smoking everyone at air hockey."

I followed her toward the sound of music cranked in the garage. A dart game between Monica's brother Charlie and Alex Mifflin was going on in one corner of the garage. I looked away, suddenly embarrassed by the memory of how close Jesse had stood while giving me dart pointers.

In the other corner, Jesse and Drew Chernov were bent over the air-hockey table, their faces intent at slamming the puck back and forth. As if these two didn't get enough hockey already.

Jesse made a fast move and sank the puck in Drew's end of the table.

"Damn it!" Drew slapped the edge of the table.

Jesse raised his arms and gave an evil-mastermind laugh. "Is there no one who can challenge me?"

I saw a spark of annoyance in Drew's eyes. Sore loser.

"You've played everyone," Drew said.

"Not Winter," Monica, beside me, said.

I stared at her with embarrassment—I hated being in the spotlight. Only when Drew gave a derisive snort did I find myself heading toward the table. Only when I'd grasped the pusher did I meet Jesse's eyes.

"Hey," he said. "Glad you could make it."

"Wait until *after* the game to say that." I had no idea where that attitude came from, but it won me a few hoots from the crowd.

Jesse smiled, and the beauty of it hit me with unexpected force. I knew I was in danger of embarrassing myself. He placed the puck in front of his pusher. "Game on, then."

I'd played air hockey before, but it'd been a few years, so I was surprised by how well I did. In fact, I scored first.

"Oohhhh!" the guys in the room, almost all members of the Tundra/Jasperton team, said in unison.

I couldn't help the smile that stretched my lips. It felt foreign, but nice. I still wasn't used to smiling again.

"Ah, I see I underestimated you," Jesse said.

The beat of the music and the desire to shove one of the pucks down Drew's throat drove me, and I scored again. Of course, then Jesse tied it up within thirty seconds.

The slap back and forth got faster and faster, the ribbing of Jesse by his teammates louder each time I sank a puck.

I had no idea how much time had elapsed, but when

I sank the final puck to win, I jumped up and actually screamed. That's when I noticed the garage was a lot fuller than when we'd begun. It looked like everyone in the house had filed in to watch our game.

I placed my pusher on the table just as Brenda called from the other room: "Pizza's here!"

As people started vacating the room in search of gooey cheese and zesty pepperoni, Jesse sat his own pusher on the table. "You're a shark," he said, then laughed.

"Too bad we weren't playing for money."

Like everyone else, I grabbed my pizza and milled about, talking.

Soon after we finished the pizza, someone tossed Jesse one of his presents.

Ten minutes into the unwrapping, I felt like I was going to pass out. Every package revealed something I hadn't bought for Jesse—a gag gift. In light of Grocery Checker Barbie and the homemade *Guide to Tundra Nightlife*—the cover of which was illustrated with a pole-dancing, lipstick-wearing moose in high highs—my present was too much, especially since Mom hadn't purchased a simple tee. Suddenly, the Canucks jersey seemed like a gift a girlfriend would give. At the very least, I didn't want him to open it in front of every- one camped out in his living room.

But it was too late. The gift was already in the pile, wedged between others. There was no way I could surrepti- tiously snatch it and run.

As the gifts dwindled, I couldn't take it anymore. I couldn't watch the reactions of my classmates, but I was on the wrong side of the room to escape. Roughly a quarter of Tundra's high school students stood between the door and me. Left with little option, I eased my way up the stairs and hid in the bathroom. I'd go back downstairs when I was sure all the presents had been opened and everyone was back to partying. Then I could slip out the door with little notice and continue hiding at my house.

I must have been a pathetic image, sitting there on the closed toilet, trying to estimate how long it would take Jesse to open the remaining presents. Timing was crucial. Why had I allowed myself to think coming to this party was a good idea? It clearly wasn't. This had to be my punishment. I was already dreading Patrice's reaction when she found out what I'd given Jesse.

The minutes stretched like an unbreakable rubber band, but eventually the music level went up. I stood, taking a deep breath and preparing my escape.

I eased out of the bathroom and started down the hall-way. That's when I heard the voices. Curious, I inched closer to a bedroom door, which was partially cracked.

Patrice stood in Jesse's room with her shirt unbuttoned and running her hands up his chest. Jesse noticed me, but I quickly averted my eyes. That's when I saw the blue, green, and white of the Canucks jersey thrown on his bed.

"Excuse me," I said as calmly as possibly, confused by how upset I was. I walked at a normal pace down the rest of the short hallway, ignoring the "Wait!" Jesse had called out. I was afraid he'd seen the disappointment in my eyes and taken it the wrong way. It was his business whom he dated, though I thought he could do better than Patrice. That was the root of my disappointment. It wasn't that I liked him. Because I didn't!

The twisting of my heart and the pounding in my head threatened to convince me I was lying to myself.

I quickened my stride, but it still took centuries to reach the stairs. When I did reach them, I hurried toward the door. My brain was functioning enough for me to grab my coat before I headed out into the cold. I had to get away. I didn't belong here.

Patrice had won. She'd snapped her fingers and gotten Jesse back, just like she'd predicted. And I had to convince myself I didn't care. After all, why should I care?

Enough of my common sense remained that I didn't run. That would just instigate even more gossip. I wondered if Mom and Dad would consider sending me away to boarding school for the rest of my senior year.

The decision not to run came back to bite me in the butt when Jesse caught up with me. I had just stepped onto my front porch and was beating the snow off the bottom of my shoes.

"Hey!"

I let any emotion fall from my face before I turned toward him. "You're not wearing a coat."

"I was in a hurry," he said. Then, after a beat: "That wasn't what you thought."

"What wasn't?"

"Don't play dumb, Winter."

"You and Patrice making out? Jesse, seriously, that's none of my business."

He frowned. "We weren't making out."

I couldn't help it; I raised my eyebrows.

"We weren't," he insisted. "She showed up—uninvited I might add—wanting to get back together. But I don't want to. And she doesn't, either—not for me anyway. It's a control thing with her. She likes to get whatever she wants."

I shoved my ungloved hands into my pockets. "She has a pretty good track record of getting exactly that."

"Not this time." The intensity in his dark eyes made me want to believe him. I just didn't know if I could, or whether I should care one way or the other.

"Why did you date her?"

He sighed and looked up at the sky. "Will you think I'm a creep if I say because she's pretty? At least at first. That, and the fact that our parents are good friends; they kind of pressured us together." He lowered his gaze back to mine and shrugged. "She's not all bad. She's capable of showing genuine caring sometimes, but . . ." He hesitated, shifted as he looked back toward his house. "I'm not saying this excuses her behavior, because it doesn't, but her parents put a crazy amount of pressure on her."

"Please don't tell me the poor-little-rich-girl story."

He shoved his hands in his jeans pockets. "Even if it's partially true?"

I stared, then finally shrugged.

"She has to be perfect, for some crazy reason. They want her to get all A's, be popular, be the best at cheering, date who they think is the best potential boyfriend. She's so busy trying to live the life her parents want that she doesn't even know what she wants herself."

"Oh, I can tell you what that is. She wants you."

Jesse took a few steps closer. "You know I don't want to get back with her. I want someone else."

The memory of our near kiss warmed my chilled, exposed cheeks. I shook my head. "I . . . I can't." Nerves caused me to stammer and take a step back before I pulled myself together. "Plus, it doesn't make sense. Guys like you end up with girls like Patrice."

"Patrice and I are over, Winter. She'll get the message. By the time we broke up, we were staying together out of habit more than anything. And that's the ugly truth." He sounded embarrassed by his admission.

Somehow I managed to keep up my ambivalent facade. I stood there, stiff, unable to force my feet to retreat as I watched Jesse climb the porch stairs, bringing his face level with mine.

"I really liked the jersey," he said.

My breath formed a little cloud as it met the cold air. "I didn't know it was a gag-gift party."

"I'm glad you didn't get me a gag gift." He lifted his hand and placed his palm against my cheek. Despite the fact that he was standing outside without a coat and gloves, his skin felt warm against mine. "It was the best present I got."

I didn't respond. I couldn't. No appropriate response formed in my head.

He looked at me another moment before sighing and

giving me a sad smile. Even faced with his disappointment, I couldn't think clearly enough to speak. I resisted the intoxicating, confusing urge to lean forward and see what might happen. While I was busy resisting temptation, he retreated down the steps and jogged back to his house and his guests. Something twisted in the pit of my stomach as I worried that he might be changing his mind about Patrice.

"There is no remedy for love but to love more."
—*Henry David Thoreau, Quote-a-Day calendar*

CHAPTER
24

"*How* was the party?" Mom asked when I stepped in.

"Fine." I even managed not to sound as shaken as I felt.

Dad lowered the medical journal he was reading. "You're home early."

"All partied out, I guess." I gestured toward the stairs. "Gotta do some homework."

When I reached my room, I stood in the dark, my back against the door, eyes closed. What was wrong with me? Why was I upset about the scene between Patrice and Jesse? Why had I felt the need to give in to kissing him? Was it pure loneliness, or was I developing real feelings for him? Feelings that were independent of Spencer or my loss of him. If so, how was it possible, so soon after Spencer's death?

I opened my eyes and listened. The faint beat of the music next door filtered through my window, preventing me from forgetting that I'd even stepped foot into the party.

As I pushed away from the door, I tried to imagine what Spencer would say if he could see me now and feel my struggle. I stopped and gasped when I couldn't recall the sound of his voice. Bits of him were slipping away. How was that possible, to know someone for years and then have the sound of his voice fade from memory in less than two months? When I could still feel him with me at times?

"Spencer?" I whispered. I scanned the room, wishing he'd somehow appear and speak to me, but nothing out of the ordinary revealed itself.

I sank onto my bed and scooted back to the headboard. I wrapped my arms around my knees and tried to pick my way through my confusion. My feelings for Jesse were jumbled, and my constant sense that Spencer wasn't totally gone didn't make it less confusing.

God, I wanted to be about thirty now, with all of this pain and confusion far behind me.

From my vantage point, I could see the light spilling from Jesse's house. Trying to focus on something else, I pulled the new costume book from the Tundra Books bag. I'd been so excited when I'd ordered it, as I'd waited for it to arrive. But when it'd finally shown up in Tundra, costume design had seemed like a frivolous dream. I hadn't even cracked the spine.

I ran my hand over the white cover, then flicked on the lamp attached to my headboard. I took a deep breath before I opened the cover. My eyes filled when I looked at the empty page where normally Spencer would have scrawled a note: some insight, something sweet, sometimes a snarky comment. I ran my fingertips over that blank page, as if they might make his words appear.

As I flipped through the pages, I remembered how Spencer used to tease me that someday I'd make the tabloids for my wild Hollywood lifestyle. I concentrated, trying to remember exactly how his voice had sounded, but only a vague echo surfaced.

I covered my face with my hands. "Oh, Spencer. I'm so sorry. Why can't I hear you anymore?"

Only the dulled sound of music from next door answered me.

I took the costume book and moved to my overstuffed chair in the corner. I lost myself in the book, in the Academy Award–winning designs of Deborah Nadoolman Landis and the history of Hollywood costume design. With each page I turned, the spark of interest in returning to my own designs grew. I'd thought the desire to draw had disappeared forever in the weeks after Spencer's crash.

A lump formed in my throat when I crossed the room to my desk and touched the cover of my sketchbook. A strange warmth surrounded me, and I imagined it was Spencer nudging me. It felt wonderful to be inspired again.

I took the sketch pad and my drawing pencils back to the chair, placing them on the ottoman. Five minutes of staring had passed before I grabbed the pad and flipped it open quickly, as though I was ripping off a Band-Aid.

But when my pencil tip touched the clean white page, instinct took over. And the first thing I created was a dress for Lindsay for the Snow Ball, because I was sure Caleb would ask her. They'd be the most stunning couple there. I made note of the fabric and supplies I'd need to create this thing of beauty—the shimmery red dress I'd originally planned for myself—and glanced at my untouched sewing machine in the corner.

After that, my pencil sprouted wings. I continued to draw and draw and draw. I drew until the cramping in my hand forced me to stop. Only then did I realize that many hours had passed, that it was the middle of the night. Next door, all was quiet and dark.

The sketching had freed something inside me, something that had been wound tight. With its release, a calm had begun taking up residence inside me. I stared at the dark house next door and decided not to stress so much about what I might feel for Jesse. I'd just take it slow and see what happened. After all, I might be stressing for no reason. Nothing might come of it.

I supposed I'd have to hang my life on a cliché and take things one day at a time.

"Where there is love there is life."
—*Mohandas K. Gandhi, Quote-a-Day calendar*

CHAPTER 25

Snow covered more and more of the mountains each day. Today, I could tell a new blanket was falling when I looked out the window of Mom's car as she drove me from school to Oregano's. I'd stuck around helping her clean up her class-room after school, aiming to ask her advice about Jesse. But something had kept me from voicing my questions.

"Will you be home for dinner?" Mom asked as she pulled into a spot in front of Oregano's. "You've got to be getting tired of the menu here."

"I don't know. I'll give you a call."

Mom didn't look at me as if I might break anymore, but I could still tell she often thought of Spencer when she watched my expressions. She reached across and patted my hand before I slipped out into the mid-October cold.

As soon as I stepped inside, Lindsay pulled me into the kitchen, past where Casey was making a Mega Cheese pizza.

"Guess what!" Lindsay looked like she might go all pogo stick any moment.

"Caleb asked you to the Snow Ball."

Her face fell. "How'd you know?"

I smiled wide. "I had a feeling he'd ask."

"Well, moose poop. Here I was anticipating springing the news on you."

I hugged her. "I'm still excited for you, Linds."

"What about you?" she asked as she pulled away. "You going to go with Jesse?"

I glanced out toward the booth where Caleb and Jesse were sitting. It had become a second home to the four of us in the past few weeks. "He hasn't asked."

"But he might have, if you'd let him."

I fiddled with a Parmesan container on one of the metal prep counters. "I know. But at the time, the very thought scared me. I didn't want to have any thought for someone other than Spencer."

"And now?"

I leaned back against the wall. "Part of me would like to go, but part of me keeps focusing on how the dance is still so tied up with Spencer."

I might daydream about Jesse, but Spencer still lived in my heart. I still ached for what might have been.

"Well, if the opportunity to go with Jesse arises again, take it," Lindsay said.

I watched Jesse talk to Caleb, their words inaudible. Would I say yes if he asked? Or was it a moot point, since I'd dodged the opportunity? Should I just ask him?

I tried to think of things other than Jesse and the Snow Ball as I headed to our usual booth. Jesse made it difficult when he smiled at me, the way he always did. He stood and allowed me to slide into the booth next to him.

We immersed ourselves in homework and bread sticks.

"What do you think is going to be on the history mid-term?" Caleb asked.

"Lots of dates," Jesse answered.

"There's always a lot of emphasis on tribal cultures," I added.

We tossed out other possibilities until we had a list of topics we thought we should focus on.

After a few minutes, I had the misfortune of looking out the window just as Patrice, Skyler, and a couple other girls walked into view. I'd given up worrying about Patrice and the angry looks she still gave me, ones that had grown darker after the night of Jesse's birthday party. It simply wasn't worth the effort. That didn't mean I wasn't aware of her sharp stares. She clearly still thought Jesse was her personal property.

Despite her obvious dislike for me, what Jesse had shared about her parents had stuck with me. Each time I caught her staring, I looked for some hint of a girl who was hurting instead of a mean girl looking for the perfect way to get back at me. I didn't know if she was hiding it deeper than before, or if the situation with Jesse had her leaning more toward the nasty end of the spectrum, but I rarely saw evidence of her gentler side. I sure didn't see it now as her eyes met mine through the glass.

"Great. She looks happy," I mumbled.

The others glanced outside, but Patrice and her friends were already coming in the front door. Instead of a viper-ish look, she'd pasted on a big smile. Trying a new tactic. Obvious much?

Jesse cursed under his breath as they approached our table. He'd shared the details of how Patrice kept calling him, leaving notes in his locker, and how she'd even started rumors that they were getting back together. Because he was a good guy and believed there was some good in her, he'd tried to discourage her without being mean. But his patience was wearing thin.

"Do you all need to order something?" Lindsay asked Patrice and her friends without getting up.

"No. You all just looked so cozy in here, we decided to come see what was up." She looked directly at me, even smiled.

I lifted my history book. "An exciting night of homework." Which should be obvious by the textbooks and notes spread all over the table.

"So what do you think will be on the history midterm?" Patrice asked as she slid into the booth next to Jesse.

I felt his body tense as he pressed up against me. What I tried to ignore was the spark of awareness that went through me when our bodies touched.

"We have no idea," Lindsay said.

"Not a clue," I added, feeling a little guilty as I said it.

When Patrice's cell rang, she glanced at the caller ID and her face fell. "Why does she have to call me a million times a day?" she muttered. She stood and walked away to answer. "Hey, Mom," she said, in a chipper voice.

Just when I'd thought Jesse had been wrong about Patrice, I saw a hint of frustration that didn't look like it had anything to do with getting her own way. Were her parents really controlling every aspect of her life?

Were they the ones urging her to get Jesse back? I tried to read more of her expression and body language to see if *she* really wanted Jesse back. But she didn't reveal much if anything was there to be revealed.

Jesse shut his book and notebook and leaned toward me. "Come on. Let's get out of here."

I needed no more prompting. I might not be worrying about Patrice anymore, but that didn't mean I wanted to hang out with her, either. I didn't feel sorry for abandoning Lindsay and Caleb, because I knew as soon as Jesse left, Patrice wouldn't stick around.

When we reached the beginning of our street, I looked back just to make sure we weren't being pursued. "Not the most graceful of getaways," I said.

"No, but it worked." Jesse swung his arm around my shoulders.

Not so long ago, I would have immediately stepped away. Now, I didn't. I didn't even try to convince myself that I just wanted his warmth to shield me from the cold. He didn't release me until we were almost to my house.

"Did you see the look on her face when her mom called?" I asked.

"No."

"It reminded me of what you told me before, about her parents pressuring her." I didn't want to be spiteful, even if I didn't like Patrice much.

Jesse stepped in front of me, and though there was no sign that things were about to change between us, my nerves sparked to life anyway.

"You're a good person, Winter Craig."

I scrunched my eyebrows. "Why do you say that?"

"Because in your position, most people wouldn't care why Patrice lashes out at people she sees as threats."

So he knew all about her actions toward me. Not surprising.

"I'm not saying we're going to become best pals or anything. I just wondered about it, that's all."

Jesse paced a couple of steps to the right. "Thing is, Patrice needs to stand up to her parents, and she doesn't. She likes being the center of attention. In some ways, she's like a two-year-old. She sees, she wants, she throws a tantrum if she doesn't get."

"And you're what she wants."

"Apparently. At least until she had me. Then she started wanting something else."

I watched the play of emotions on Jesse's face and braved a question everyone had been asking since his and Patrice's breakup. "Do you think she slept with someone else?"

He shrugged. "Maybe, maybe not. I can see it being a little rebellion against her parents. Doesn't really matter now."

"I'm sorry."

Jesse's gaze met mine, and the way he looked at me—with a yearning for something real—tugged at my heart. My mouth opened to ask him what I'd not allowed him to ask me that night at his house. But again, something stopped me. Fear, uncertainty, Spencer's continued presence in my heart—I wasn't sure. Part of me was angry at myself for not having the strength to leave Spencer's memory behind, while another part was still desperate to hold on to my loyalty.

How long would this battle continue?

I wondered if Jesse sensed my struggle, because he gave me a half smile and glanced toward the center of town.

"See you tomorrow. I'm going in, just in case Patrice's posse decides to pick up their game," he said with a wink.

I climbed my porch steps but hesitated at the door. Instead of going inside, I stood in the shadows and watched Jesse walk to his house. This semidarkness seemed the only place I could admit, even to myself, that beneath the layer of friendship, I was feeling something else for him. A yearning that matched what I'd seen in his eyes.

Should I tell him before it was too late, as had happened with Spencer? Would I ever be fully ready?

I sighed and went inside, wishing I knew the way to answer my own questions.

"A kiss is a lovely trick designed by nature to stop speech when words become superfluous."
—Ingrid Bergman, Quote-a-Day calendar

CHAPTER

26

Saturday dawned bright but colder than normal for October. Still, there was no missing the annual fall craft fair at Town Park. It always provided one of the better chances to buy Christmas gifts without having to order them from Anchorage. As usual, the Snow Ball committee was having a bake sale, and Mom had made her famous three-tiered red-velvet cake as a contribution. And even though I still didn't know if I'd attend the dance, I'd whipped up some pumpkin bars and lemon squares to donate.

Mom and I carried our sugary offerings to the square. The crowd was already visible as soon as we reached the front of our lot. The craft fair was the one time of the year when you could guarantee seeing people who didn't poke their heads out any other time. Many of them were crafts-men in addition to being hermits, and this was when they made the bulk of their money. The timing worked out well. They could sell their creations and stock up on provisions for the winter in one trip.

With winter just around the corner, the fair also provided

people with the chance to enjoy each other's company before the weather became too dangerous to travel.

Luck was not with me, however, as we approached the Snow Ball booth. Patrice sat right in the middle of the table, smiling as if she'd already been crowned Snow Ball Queen. Despite what I now knew about her relationship with her parents, she still grated on my last nerve.

"Winter, hey!" she said, startling me so much I nearly dropped my containers of sweets. "Good to see you. Hi, Mrs. Craig."

"Patrice. We've got a few things for you."

"Great. We can use all the donations we can get. I think this is going to be the best Snow Ball ever."

A pang tugged at my heart. It would have been the best Snow Ball ever.

Mom smiled as she set down the cake. Even she looked a bit surprised by Patrice's brightness, made even brighter by her canary-yellow coat and cute knitted hat. Frothy. She looked frothy. Behind the overt friendliness, though, I sensed something darker lurking. Unwilling to stick around to find out if I was right, I turned to follow Mom through the crowd.

"Whore."

I stopped and looked over my shoulder. Had I heard what I'd just thought I'd heard? Though Patrice smiled and waved, my skin crawled.

By the time I found Lindsay and we'd strolled through several booths, however, I let the suspicions about Patrice go. She was so not going to spoil a good day for me. I'd always loved the fall craft fair—the carvings, the photographs of Alaskan wildlife and scenery, the funnel cakes and fry bread, the jelly beans game always sponsored by Shaggy's Trading Post. Each year, Shaggy put the jelly beans in a different type of container, so the previous year's correct number didn't help anyone.

Lindsay and I met up with Caleb just before we reached Shaggy's booth. I was already calculating what I'd do with the two-hundred-dollar prize, when the people in front of me moved out of the way to reveal this year's container.

"Ew," Lindsay said as she looked at the man's hiking boot filled to the top with jelly beans.

"It's a new boot, Linds," I said. "Besides, they're not for eating."

After we'd made our guesses, we headed for the food area that ran from Chow's down the road to the grocery. On the way, a carving of a moose caught my attention. Dad loved moose, had them all over his office. This might be a great piece to add to his collection.

"I'll catch up with you guys in a few minutes."

Caleb and Lindsay nodded and kept walking hand in hand toward the fattening and wonderful fair foods.

As I approached the booth, I caught a group of sophomores watching me. When I met their gazes, they looked away and started whispering. What was that about? Surely not the jersey fiasco? Jesse had explained that away by saying that I actually hadn't picked out the gift. I shook my head. Whatever.

I examined the large moose carving with its intricate

detail, then balked at the price tag. Even if I won the jelly-bean contest, this was still out of my limited price range.

"Hey, Winter."

I turned to find Monica looking at me with a tight expression on her face.

"What's wrong?"

She scanned the area around us and pulled me away from a group of men talking about a recent caribou hunt.

"I thought you should know what's going around."

"What do you mean?"

She gave me a pained expression. "I just heard the rumor that you've slept with not one but both of Lindsay's older brothers, and that now you're going after Jesse."

My mouth dropped open. "That's not true! Any of it!" I might be attracted to Jesse, but I wasn't "after him."

"I know. I just thought I should tell you before it spread any farther."

Patrice. My fists clenched beside me. I couldn't believe I'd ever felt any empathy for her. I was going to rip off her head and stick it on a spike, cute little knit hat and all.

Sometimes you had to fight mean with mean.

I stalked through the crowd, bumping into people and not bothering to apologize. This nonsense with Patrice was ending today, one way or another.

"Hey, Winter," Patrice said as I approached. "Want something sweet to eat?"

"No, Patrice, I want you to stop spreading lies about me just because you can't convince Jesse to take you back."

My attack must have surprised her because she looked

around frantically, probably worrying that I was going to reveal the girl behind the goody-two-shoes mask to everyone else. Not a bad idea, come to think of it.

"I don't know what you're talking about."

"Stop lying. Everyone knows you're the one who started the rumor that I've been sleeping around." I spit the words at her like acid.

Her eyes narrowed. "Rumors often have a basis in fact."

"Then that must mean you cheated on Jesse. People whisper about it. Therefore, it must be true."

Patrice rose and stared hard at me. "Then it must also be true that those nasty Kusagak boys weren't enough for you, so you had to sneak out to seduce poor Spencer Isaacs in the middle of the night. The night before he crashed."

"Shut up, Patrice!" Jesse's voice. "Just shut up."

The world spun as Patrice frantically hissed back at Jesse to be quiet. I stumbled backward, unable to breathe. Spencer's crash. What if he'd been too tired to fly? What if he hadn't been focused because of me and my late-night visit?

What if it was all my fault?

I turned and ran blindly, with no idea where I was going.

I ran until my lungs screamed for mercy, until my tears and the chilled air chapped my cheeks. When I slipped on the gravel lining the trail along the river, I fell to my knees and stayed down. I sucked in air until my breathing approached normal before I moved. I ignored the stinging of my knees as I pulled myself to sit halfway down the riverbank.

What a beautiful day to feel like the world was falling apart. The tundra blazed red and gold, and a few fly fishermen lined the opposite side of the river, casting for hungry rainbow trout. And here I sat in the dirt, the hole inside me growing larger and darker with each passing moment.

Why had I gone to Spencer's that night, when I knew he should be getting his rest? Fresh tears tracked down my cheeks, and I laid my forehead against my upturned knees. I cried until I made myself sick. I was tempted to curl up in the brush and stay there until I ceased to exist.

Footsteps crunched on the gravel, heading my way. I wiped the lingering tears away with the sleeve of my coat.

"There you are." Jesse sounded relieved. He scrambled down the riverbank to my side. "Are you okay?"

I opened my mouth to say I was fine, but that wasn't what came out. "No." My voice broke. I doubted I'd ever be okay again.

Jesse wiped away my fresh tears. I saw with my blurry vision that he was upset, his face tightened like he wanted to throttle someone. My guess was Patrice.

"You can't listen to her," he said.

"But what if she's right?" The mere thought slashed at my insides like an angry raptor's claws. "What if something I did? . . ."

Jesse shook me. Not hard, but enough to get my attention. "Don't think like that. You had nothing to do with what happened to Spencer. The plane stalled. You know that. Patrice has just gone too far. There's no excuse for that."

I looked into Jesse's dark eyes. It seemed impossible that

he was here with me, taking my side. The world truly had turned upside down.

"I've never done anything to her, nothing to make her hate me this much." I looked down at the torn knees of my jeans. "I'm never going to be able to face anyone again." I inhaled a shuddery breath. Maybe I could disappear into the bush, try my hand at living off the land, follow the grand tradition of Alaskan hermits.

I didn't resist when Jesse pulled me against him. His chest felt warm and safe.

"You don't have to worry about that."

"But she said those things where everyone could hear her. I'm sure the entire borough knows by now."

He ran his hand slowly over my hair, which had fallen loose from its clip. "Not as many people heard as you might think. Besides, what they know is that Patrice is a liar, and that she strikes out like a snake when she doesn't get her way."

I pulled back and stared at him. "You said that?"

He nodded. "I put up with her little games because part of me felt sorry for her. I thought maybe she'd grow up and get a backbone. But what she said to you was too much."

"Thank you." I still worried that the damage was done. Once something was even whispered in Tundra, everyone heard about it—whether it was true or not. That Jesse had taken up for me was huge. My heart, which had sat so cold and heavy in my chest moments before, warmed.

"You want to go back?"

I shook my head. "I think I'm done with the craft fair

for this year." Maybe forever, since I'd likely not be here at this time next year. I hated Patrice for ruining it for me, for breathing the possibility that Spencer's death was my fault.

I just couldn't face everyone so soon after the scene with Patrice. I was afraid they'd see me differently.

I expected Jesse to leave. Instead, he scooted closer, wrapping his arm around my shoulders and planting a soft kiss on my head. This time, the kiss might have been meant as comfort, but my heart fluttered that it might lead to more.

"If I know what love is, it is because of you."
—*Herman Hesse, Quote-a-Day calendar*

CHAPTER

27

Jesse was right—at least partially. Come Monday morning, I sensed only the occasional whisper or curious look as I walked down the school hallway. As for Patrice, she ignored my existence, which was probably the best reaction I could hope for. That—combined with the fact that I'd spent Sunday being assured by Jesse and Lindsay that I had nothing to do with Spencer's death—had moved my mood up from ghastly to slightly less ghastly.

I stuffed my books into my locker. When I closed the door, Lindsay stood there with a wide grin.

"Well, hello, Smiley McSmilerson."

"I have great news for you."

"Yeah?"

"I just overheard Patrice talking to her little posse in the restroom, and she said that the Snow Ball committee is hosting an impromptu final fund-raiser on Halloween to bring in a DJ from Kodiak."

"And this is good news for me how?"

"It's a *costume* contest, one that Patrice is bragging she's going to win! She's already asked her aunt in Anchorage to get her a really hot vampire outfit from a costume shop there. But any of your designs could *smoke* something she gets from a rental shop."

A little thrill zipped through me, but I reined it in. "I don't want to perpetuate this thing with Patrice."

"No one has to know," Lindsay said, a wickedly joyful conspiracy thick in her voice. "Think how good it would feel to take her down a notch yourself, with your talent."

We'd talked about this the day before. While she thought it was really heroic of Jesse to do what he had, she'd also said I needed to make my own stand against Patrice and let go of my worry over why she acted the way she did. Maybe this way I could take that stand without punching her in the face. A bit of self-satisfaction without causing a scene.

"Okay, but only if you do it, too."

"Deal." She said it before my words were fully out of my mouth, as if she thought I'd back out. "We'll get to work on it this afternoon, when I get out of practice."

I couldn't wait that long. When I should have been taking notes in my classes, I doodled possible designs. Historical costume was my specialty, though I dabbled with other themes from time to time. While I liked some of my ideas, nothing said, "This is it!"

By the time Lindsay showed up at my house after basketball practice, I had sketches strewn all over my room. She scooted a batch out of the way and flopped onto her stomach on my bed. She flipped through several possibilities while I flicked my pencil against my sketch pad's spiral binding.

"These are all good. What are you leaning toward?"

"I don't know. None of them feel right. I want something more . . . aggressive."

Lindsay looked up. "Sort of a 'my costume character can kick your costume character's butt' kind of thing."

I smiled. "Yeah."

"So a superhero." She hopped from the bed and booted up my computer, doing a Web search for female superheroes.

Still, nothing struck me. Seriously, I wouldn't wear some of those skimpy costumes even if it weren't late October in Alaska. Just as I was about to give up, our Web surfing stumbled upon Illyria, a superpowerful demon turned good girl from the TV show *Angel*.

"Of course! Illyria was totally badass," I said. Linds and I had watched *Angel* and *Buffy the Vampire Slayer* religiously with Mom and my sisters when we were younger.

"Her costume is awesome," Lindsay said as she pointed at the deep reds and blues of the tight leather bodysuit. Then she looked at me. "Plus, you look a little like Fred." Fred being the brainy girl whose body Illyria took over when she was released from her sarcophagus.

"Scoot." I shooed Lindsay out of my desk chair and did a bit of surfing until I found a store in Anchorage where I could order the materials I needed. I put a next-day rush on the order, which meant I'd have to set my clock early in the morning so I could call Charlie at the airport before he or Harry Logan made a supply run to Anchorage.

"Now all I need is a blond wig, a Buffy shirt and a wooden stake, and I can stake Patrice's skanky vamp," Lindsay said.

I snorted at the image and immediately started surfing

for Buffy gear. Within five minutes I'd ordered those items, too.

"I'll pay you for those when I get paid next time," Lindsay told me.

I gave her my don't-start-this-silliness look. "Come on, I'd pay twice that to see native Buffy chasing down Patrice."

Her bark of laughter made me smile, a definite up on the roller-coaster ride my life had become in recent weeks.

"Dinner's ready," Mom called up the stairs.

When we reached the kitchen, I skidded to a halt, causing Lindsay to run into me. Jesse sat at the table.

"Hey," he said.

"Hey."

"I ran into Jesse outside," Mom said as she ladled stew into bowls. "His parents are over in Dillingham tonight, so I invited him to dinner."

I shifted from one foot to the other. This wasn't awkward *at all*. Even after talking to him over the weekend, I felt a bit weird around him. I was still addled by that kiss he'd placed on my head and the way he'd held me as I'd cried after my fight with Patrice. The way my body had reacted to his nearness, his touch, by increasing my pulse and urging me closer.

We managed to get through dinner with normal, non-embarrassing conversation. Afterward, Linds, Jesse, and I flopped in front of the TV and put *Underworld* in the DVD player.

"Are you two entering the costume contest?" Jesse asked.

"Yes." Lindsay slid down on the couch and propped her feet against the sturdy wooden coffee table my parents had purchased at a fall craft fair when I was three. "We just ordered the stuff before dinner. It rocks to have a designer as a best friend."

Jesse's eyes met mine. "What are you dressing up as?"

"It's a surprise." I tried to focus on Kate Beckinsale and not on how she looked way better in her catsuit than I was going to look in my costume. "Are you entering?"

"I'll be too busy wearing my uniform."

I looked back at him. "Huh?"

"Oh, the contest is at the hockey game against Kenai," Lindsay piped up without looking away from the TV.

"The hockey game?" I'd envisioned walking around the hallways of school dressed as Illyria, not strutting around the ice rink in front of half the town. "Funny how you neglected to mention that."

Lindsay gave me *the stare*. "You are so not backing out on me now. Besides, you already ordered the stuff."

What had I gotten myself into? And just so I could have my little fantasy of beating Patrice in a costume contest.

Mom came in with a bowl of popcorn, placed it on the coffee table, then looked at the TV. "He's hot." She whistled low. "He" being Scott Speedman as he was being chased by Lycans.

"Mom!" Was there anything worse than having your mother acknowledge a guy's hotness in front of a guy your own age?

She turned, winked at us, and left the room. Was she

winking because she was reveling in my embarrassment, or did she think something was going on with Jesse? How could she suspect that when I didn't even know what was going on?

Left alone, the three of us ate popcorn, and Jesse added a running commentary to the movie. Lindsay and I took turns shushing him. When Kate Beckinsale's character, Selene, had to bite Scott Speedman's Michael, Jesse said, "She could bite me anytime."

"She doesn't like guys who talk through movies," I said.

He tossed popcorn at me just as I leaned forward to pick more from the bowl. His shot hit me in the ear. Without missing a beat, some buried part of my personality surged to the surface. "You come into my house and throw food at me?" I hurled a handful of popcorn at him. Thus ensued a good two minutes of popcorn mayhem until I noticed Mom standing in the doorway to the kitchen, arms crossed. She didn't look particularly upset.

She shook her head. "Have fun cleaning it up. And make sure you all get your homework done." With that, she turned and walked down the hallway to her bedroom.

Lindsay snorted as she grabbed the now-empty bowl and started filling it with popcorn from the floor and couch. By the time we'd finished, the vampire elder had begun to awaken, signaling a sequel.

After taking the bowl into the kitchen to dump its contents in the garbage, my sneaky friend headed up the stairs. "Got to write a paper."

I happened to know that her paper for English comp was

done already. I stared at her with a pleading expression, but she just smiled and disappeared.

Awk-ward.

"It's good to see you laugh." Jesse watched me from his perch on the love seat, his long arms spread across the back.

I pulled my legs up onto the couch and wrapped my arms around them. "It still feels weird. Wrong, sometimes."

"It's not wrong. You have the right to keep living. No one expects you never to have fun again."

"But it seems too soon. Spencer hasn't even been gone two months."

"There's no timetable for grieving. I remember my grandmother telling my dad that sometime after Mom left."

Maybe he was right. Perhaps I would have some good days with bad ones thrown in. I wondered when the guilt over those good times would end. Maybe, without realizing it, I was already having more good days than bad.

"I guess."

Jesse waited another beat before getting to his feet. "I better go do my own paper. I think I have about twelve words on what makes William Shakespeare's work so important. Of course, I have to go make up some stuff, since Shakespeare puts me to sleep."

Though his words should have made me sad, I actually laughed. "Spencer hated Shakespeare, too. Inside my cover of *A Midsummer Night's Dream*, he wrote, 'A Midsummer Night's Snore.'"

"I like that. Maybe I'll call my paper 'Shakespeare: A Sure Cure for Insomnia.'"

"Yeah, I'm thinking the grade for that equals 'Not so hot.'"

He sighed dramatically. "Fine. Off to write a bunch of lies, then."

I didn't expect a good-night kiss, especially since I'd rebuffed his earlier attempt, but his departure left me feeling adrift. I stood in the empty living room for several minutes, reexamining my unexpected feelings for Jesse.

Before I drove myself nuts, I headed for the stairs. I had some payback to dish out. I had a dozen tactics floating in my head when I opened my bedroom door to find Lindsay in front of the mirror. She was examining the fading bruise on her cheek. The deep purple had faded to a lighter shade, and part of it had begun turning yellow. She jumped back from the mirror.

I wanted to ask if she'd heard anything about her father, but I figured it wasn't a topic she'd be in the mood to discuss. If she did, she'd bring it up.

"So, anything interesting to share?" Lindsay asked as she went back to the overstuffed chair where her homework was spread.

"Nothing, other than that Jesse has an undying hatred for Shakespeare."

"Too bad the flirting didn't pay off."

"Flirting?"

"Yes, you were flirting."

I stared at her, shocked. "I wasn't!"

"Whatever you say." She picked up her Alaska history book.

"I wasn't," I said again as I slid into my desk chair. Even as I said it, I wondered if I was lying to myself. Anyway, was flirting with Jesse such a bad thing?

I thought back to when I'd hit the purchase button for my costume materials. What did it say that I'd wondered more about what Jesse would think of the outfit than if it would be enough to beat Patrice's? I'd never admit it aloud, but I wanted him to think it was hotter than Patrice's vamp.

And I wanted the guilt associated with that wish to fly away.

"There is nothing holier in this life of ours than the first consciousness of love—the first fluttering of its silken wings."
—Henry Wadsworth Longfellow, Quote-a-Day calendar

CHAPTER

28

I stared at the red and blue leather clinging to my body. "There is no way I'm wearing this in public."

"Yes, you are." Lindsay leaped onto my bed, the blond hair of her wig flying as she raised her wooden stake. "Even if I have to drag you by your blue-highlighted hair."

I took another look at myself. It was a cool costume, but walking into the hockey rink wearing it made my stomach flip-flop. Maybe I'd just wear my coat the entire game and skip the contest. Really, what good would beating Patrice do anyway?

Then I thought of how she'd struck back at me by telling lies. How even Jesse standing up to her in the park hadn't cost her any friendships or admiration. Sure, winning this silly contest wouldn't make everything right again, but it'd be some small victory for me. A statement that she wasn't winning on *my* turf.

Caleb drove us the short distance to the rink. By the time he pulled into the gravel lot, I felt like I was going to be ill.

"You'll be great! Stop thinking so much," Lindsay reassured me as she slid out of the truck beside me.

When we walked inside, I noticed all kinds of costumes. The typical witches and ghosts mingled with Dr. Seuss's Thing One and Thing Two—the Shively twins—and a walking igloo. Lindsay took off her coat, revealing her Buffy outfit, which also included my cute pair of black boots. Sharing the same shoe size with your best friend had definite advantages.

Not ready to share my formfitting costume with anyone, I kept my coat firmly closed as we made our way to an empty spot in the bleachers.

"Come on, stop hiding," Lindsay said. "Your costume rocks. Why do you want to hide it?"

Caleb craned his neck around Lindsay and peered at me closely. "Yeah, what's the big mystery? Lindsay has been excited about it all week."

"Fine." I'd take off my coat if it'd stop their nagging. Might as well get it over with. People were already looking at my blue hair and lips anyway.

I heard the chatter start as soon as I stood and unzipped my coat. I nearly bolted. I tried to pull from the strength of Illyria's personality. She wouldn't care what everyone thought of her or her looks.

I pushed the sound of indistinguishable comments away as I refocused on the ice, watching Jesse skate around on the rink.

As the game started and the players began to fly across

the ice, I relaxed and reacted with the rest of the crowd. The break between the first and second periods arrived before I realized it. Then two guys rolled a long rug out onto the ice and Jakob Mueller announced, "Anyone who wants to compete in the costume contest, come on down to the ice."

Before I could balk, Lindsay grabbed my hand and dragged me down the steps leading to the ice. I spotted Patrice as we passed her. Long, shiny black wig. Blood-tipped fangs. Inky-black dress with black lace cuffs. I had to admit her outfit was going to be hard to beat.

Lindsay kept holding my hand as we took our places at the end of the line and waited for Jakob to make his way through all the contestants. I wondered if Lindsay's black-leather pants and jacket were as cold as my full-length leather ensemble.

The winner would be judged by the crowd's cheering, so I prepared myself for a loss when Patrice's cheers nearly deafened me.

The girl led a charmed life, despite what she might think.

Lindsay's Buffy outfit got a good amount of cheers, largely due to her hamming it up by pretending to stake Patrice.

"And finally, Winter Craig."

I took a step forward but nearly jumped back when the crowd erupted. I glanced at Lindsay, who gave me two thumbs-up, then motioned for the crowd to yell even louder. They did. When the noise finally died down, Jakob said, "No need for a second round on this one! The winner by several decibels . . ." A drumroll came over the rink's sound system, and I felt everyone's eyes on me. "Winter Craig."

Excitement surged through me, and it had nothing to do with Patrice. A costume I'd made had just won an award. True, it was only a twenty-dollar gift certificate to Shaggy's Trading Post, but the prize wasn't what mattered. I wondered if this was just the beginning. I smiled when I looked down at the certificate and, beyond it, noticed that the carpet they'd rolled out onto the ice was red.

I heard a disgusted huff and turned toward Patrice. I watched as she jerked the fangs out of her mouth and squeezed them tight in her fist. For one surreal moment, I thought she might cry. An empathy I'd thought she'd destroyed forever moved within me. But then she pierced me with a furious stare only I could see before stalking off the ice. Patrice wasn't used to losing, and if Jesse was right, her parents wouldn't like this streak.

I couldn't wait until Patrice Murray and her parental issues were a distant memory.

The hockey teams returned to the ice as the rest of the costume contestants started filing off. I noticed Jesse and his stunned expression when he saw me, just as he ran into the back of Drew Chernov. He struggled not to fall, and I stifled a giggle.

During the second period, satisfaction and happiness filled up some of the empty places inside me. I watched Jesse skate, slam opposing players against the boards, and score. When he got called for high-sticking and was sent to the penalty box, he looked directly at me. My skin warmed, despite the cold that emanated from the ice. I wondered if anyone could see me blush with all the white and blue makeup coating my face.

In the few moments our eyes were locked, I wondered again what it would be like to kiss him.

When his attention returned to the game and the dwindling time on the penalty, I looked down at my hands, which were clasped in my lap. Was I a horrible person, thinking about kissing Jesse? When it hadn't been that long since I'd kissed Spencer, the boy I'd wanted to love my entire life?

My joy drained away, like the water in a sink when the plug was pulled. I resisted the urge to leave. I didn't want my mood swing to ruin how much fun Lindsay and Caleb were having. But when the final buzzer blew, I was the first to stand and head toward the exit.

"Winter, wait up!"

I turned to find Jesse hurrying up the stairs, still wearing his skates.

Lindsay leaned toward me. "We'll wait for you outside."

My mind whirled in confusion. I smiled at Jesse, but it felt shaky.

"Hey. Congrats on the win," I said.

He motioned toward my costume. "I could say the same. What are you, exactly?"

I laughed a little. "Illyria. TV character from a few years ago."

"Oh. Cool."

Some people trying to leave the rink jostled Jesse, caus-

ing him to step closer to me. My breath caught in my throat
as I met his eyes and remembered the thought I'd had earlier
about kissing him. That possibility thrummed through my
veins as his eyes dropped to my lips. I could even feel myself
leaning closer.

Unfortunately—or perhaps fortunately—I spotted
Spencer's parents behind Jesse, walking toward us. I jerked
away as Mrs. Isaacs noticed me and offered that sad smile
I associated with her now. God, had she seen the yearning
between Jesse and me? What must she think of me if she
did?

Was this their first outing since Spencer's death? Guilt
gnawed at me. Their difficult first step might have brought
them only more pain because of me.

"Congratulations on your win, Winter," Mrs. Isaacs said
as she approached. She patted Jesse on the arm. "Good
game, Jesse."

"Thank you." Jesse and I said it at the same time, increasing the discomfort of the moment.

When the Isaacses headed away, I kept my gaze pointed
at the concrete floor. Thoughts of Spencer dampened my
mood again. I hated that. He'd always made me smile, laugh,
love life, and look forward to the next day. Now memories
of him made me sad, reopening the wound inside me every
time it tried to heal.

I sensed Jesse's frustration, but he reined it in, seeming
to understand. He squeezed my hand and leaned next to my
ear. "That really is a great costume."

I could tell by the way he said "great" that he thought

it was sexy, and that he wanted me to stop holding him at arm's length. I wished I could.

When I said nothing in response, he sighed and let go. "See you later." He started back down the stairs toward the rink and the locker room.

I stood and watched him until he was out of sight. I wondered if my mind and heart would ever stop spinning long enough for me to figure out what I should do. What I wanted.

"Love . . . 'Tis second life, it grows into the soul, warms every vein, and beats in every pulse."
—Joseph Addison, *Quote-a-Day calendar*

CHAPTER
29

It was really odd how thoughts of Spencer haunted me every day, while I also thought of Jesse more and more often. He hadn't made any further moves or even mentioned the near kiss. I wondered if my pulling away yet again had extinguished whatever interest had been there. My heart ached at that thought. Not the same kind of ache I felt when I thought of Spencer, but an ache nonetheless.

Even odder was how natural it felt to walk to and from school with Jesse, spend time doing homework at each other's houses, and join Caleb in attending Lindsay's basketball games. Sometimes I felt as if Spencer approved of me moving on. Others, it seemed like he was watching with disapproval from just out of sight. I didn't know which, if either, was true.

November arrived with ever-shortening days and colder temperatures. A few inches of snow blanketed the ground on one of the days when neither Lindsay nor I had to be at Oregano's after school. Because her mom had the flu, she headed straight home. I had to do some research in the school library after classes were over, so when I left, I bumped into Jesse leaving hockey practice.

"Waiting for me?" He gave me a crooked, teasing grin, the first I'd seen in a while. I felt a spurt of unexpected hope come alive.

"No, sorry. Didn't renew my groupie membership." Considering the unspoken tension that had risen between us since Halloween night, joking with him came surprisingly easily.

I headed out the door, and he followed, falling into step beside me as I walked toward the middle of town. As we passed through the main part of Tundra, we spotted Shaggy Murtough out in front of the trading post feeding Boo, his pet caribou. He'd saved Boo when she'd been a baby, after her mother was run over by a truck. Even when he'd tried to return her to the wild, she wouldn't go.

Jesse nodded in Boo's direction. "Bet you won't see something like that when you move to Hollywood."

"I don't know if I'm going there."

"That's where the movie industry is." He moved in front of me but kept walking backward. "After all, you're already an award-winning designer."

I stuck my tongue out at his teasing tone.

"Careful, that's going to freeze out here."

Lacking a witty comeback, I reached down and grabbed a handful of snow. He laughed and ran across Town Park to our street. I worked the snow into a ball as I ran after him. When it was round and solid, I slid to a stop and took aim.

"Ack!" Jesse spun around when the snowball hit him in the back and exploded. "Oh, it's on!"

I squeaked and ran toward the other side of the street. A snowball caught me on the neck just below my knitted cap. Smaller chunks slid down my neck, making me shiver.

We shrieked and bombarded each other with snowballs all the way down the street to my house. Instead of running up the front steps, I careened around the side of the house to the backyard. As I rounded the corner, Jesse tackled me.

"That's cold!" I wriggled to get loose but only managed to free one arm.

A wide smile of victory stretched across Jesse's mouth. I reached over and grabbed a handful of snow, then proceeded to rub it all over his face.

A bit more rolling and slipping brought us face-to-face. We stopped struggling, and our visible breaths puffed out between us.

"I have a question to ask you, and I don't want you avoiding it again." He sounded so matter-of-fact, as if there wasn't a charge sizzling between us.

"Okay."

"Want to go to the Snow Ball with me?"

Memories flashed of me asking Spencer to the dance, him smiling and saying yes, and me dreaming of dancing in his arms. I pushed them all away. I didn't want to feel this aching hole inside me anymore.

"Sure."

"Good."

I thought he'd release me then, but he continued to stare

down at me. When he started to lower his lips toward mine, I panicked and turned my face away. I could convince myself to go to a dance, but this . . . this I wasn't ready for. Was I?

Jesse let out a long sigh, then lifted to his feet. He offered his hand, though I could tell he was holding in barely restrained frustration. I didn't mean to be so crazed—so hot and cold—but I couldn't seem to help it. It was like I'd gone emotionally schizo or something.

Should I have said no? Should I just have cut the ties between us before we got in too deep?

Before we felt too much, and it ended badly?

"Whoso loves, believes the impossible."
—*Elizabeth Barrett Browning, Quote-a-Day calendar*

CHAPTER

30

The look of disappointment I'd seen on Jesse's face nagged at me from the moment he walked away, all through that night, and into the next morning. What was wrong with me? Why was I holding on to Spencer when there was nothing beyond memories to hold on to?

Jesse was a good guy. Nice, understanding, funny. Gorgeous. And despite how I treated him sometimes, he seemed to like me at least enough to want a kiss.

Hoping I could make it up to him, I headed to the rink, where he and the rest of the team were slamming bodies with Cold Creek. I didn't hide the fact I was cheering for him. Let everyone else think what they wanted to.

Almost an entire period went by before he noticed me. I waved and smiled. He offered a crooked smile below his visor, before skating onto the ice for another shift.

That smile made me feel better and increased my antici-pation for the end of the game. I still didn't know exactly what I might be ready for, but I had to admit I kept wondering what would have happened if I hadn't turned my face away the day before. What would Jesse's kisses be like? Though

I tried to keep my mind from venturing down the track of comparison, I couldn't stop wondering how they would measure against Spencer's. They wouldn't have the pent-up yearning that had fueled the kisses between Spencer and me. But would that make them any less enjoyable?

A new thought scared me. What if his kisses were *better* than Spencer's?

I sighed as I watched Jesse fly down the ice. I doubted his kisses would be a letdown.

As the final seconds of the game ticked off the clock, I headed out to the lobby area across from the locker room. Not so close that I looked obvious, but close enough that Jesse could see me when he came off the ice.

It worked. He wandered out of the line of players in my direction. "Hey, Winter. I saw you cheering. Thanks for being here."

"Yeah. I'm thinking of taking up cheerleading. Think Patrice will let me on the squad?"

He leaned in closer. "I swear I'll stop talking to you."

I tilted my head and pursed my lips, like I was weighing my options.

He made like he was going to tickle me, causing me to squeak and back up into an alcove next to the snack bar, which hid us from most of the people leaving the rink. My breath caught in my lungs when he lifted his hand to my cheek. This time I wasn't going to pull away. I needed to know, one way or the other.

The buzzing of my phone startled me, breaking the moment. "Sorry," I said, giving Jesse a please-forgive-me smile as I pulled the phone out of my pocket. But it wasn't a call. It was a text. Lindsay, most likely. I'd scold her later for her incredibly bad timing.

But when I looked at the display, it wasn't from Lindsay. My heart missed a beat, and I lifted my hand to my mouth to stifle a gasp.

"What is it?" Jesse asked.

I stepped around him and looked wildly around the lobby.

"Winter?"

I hurried back into the rink, but almost everyone was gone. None of the remaining faces were Spencer's.

Maybe instead of a miracle, I was hallucinating. But when I looked back at the phone, the word "PERSUASION" stared back at me, sent from Spencer's cell number. An answer to the question I'd asked him the night before he died: what to read, *The Tempest* or *Persuasion*?

Jesse took my arm until I looked up at him. "What's wrong?"

I swallowed against the dryness invading my throat. "Spencer." I held up the phone. "It's a text from Spencer."

His eyebrows knotted, as if I were talking nonsense. Was I?

No, this had to be a sign. Spencer was out there some-where, trying to reach me. The only other explanations were that this message had floated around out in the satellite ether for two months, or I was totally crazy.

"Winter." Jesse shook his head as if it were the latter.

But the message *had* to mean something. Why else

would it show up right at the moment when I was about to cast aside Spencer for someone else? Had I allowed Jesse, Lindsay, and my parents to persuade me to do exactly that?

I knew it sounded absolutely nuts, but what if there was the slimmest chance Spencer was alive? As I looked up at Jesse, at his eyes so filled with confusion and hurt, I wasn't sure how I felt about Spencer's reappearance.

I turned away as guilt slammed into me full force. How could I even think such a thing? I loved Spencer.

Without looking back at Jesse, I ran toward the doors into the cold, snowflake-laden night.

I looked at every face I passed on the way home, down every street, behind every building. By the time I got home, fear that I really *was* losing my mind had begun to grip me. Did I need to tell someone—my parents—just in case? As soon as I had the thought, I knew how it would sound coming out of my mouth. My parents would look at me the way Jesse had. As if I needed professional mental help.

But I couldn't say nothing. I had to know what this message meant. I took a deep breath and ran downstairs.

I found Dad in his office, looking over patient records.

"Hi, honey," he said, when he looked up to see me standing in the doorway. "What's up?"

I had to take another deep breath before I could move forward and speak. "I need your help."

He set down the file he was holding. "Is something wrong?"

"Yes. No." I shook my head. "I don't know." I pulled out

my phone, just to make sure the message was still there. "I got a text message tonight . . . from Spencer."

It took a couple of seconds for the stunned look on his face to dissolve into one of pity. "Sweetie, that's not possible."

I extended the phone to him. "He answered a question I asked him the night before the crash. No one else could have done that."

Dad took the phone and looked at the display. His forehead wrinkled. "You're sure this came from Spencer's number?"

"Yes." I sank into the chair across his desk from him. "I know it doesn't make sense, but . . . what if somehow he's still alive and trying to ask for help?"

Dad placed the phone atop the file he'd been reading. "I know this has been hard, honey. It's a loss someone your age shouldn't have to go through, but you have to accept that there's no way he could have survived." He said it with his gentle tone he used to deliver bad news to patients. "No way, sweetie."

He didn't delve into the details of the crash scene, but I knew he was thinking about finding the mangled, charred remains of the plane. Deep in my heart, I knew he was right. A hollowness opened up inside me.

"But the message?"

Dad looked at me with kind eyes. I could tell he wanted to get his point across without hurting me. "If he were alive and could send you a message, why wouldn't he text 'Help,' or some clue where he was?"

I stood, paced, tried to slow the insane beating of my

heart. "But no one's found Spencer. How can we be sure?" I knew I sounded desperate, verging on insane.

Dad stood slowly and rounded his desk. I backed up, not wanting comfort. I wanted the truth to not be the truth. I wanted Spencer to be alive. I wanted to talk to him again, to be able to tell him how much he really meant to me.

"The details would only hurt you, but trust me. There were no human footprints leading away from the wreckage."

Before I could say anything, Dad took the steps necessary to wrap me in his arms. I clung to him and didn't fight it as the hollowness yawned wider.

"How bright, how clear this light, . . . this love that shines out in a shadowed world."
—Pam Brown, Quote-a-Day calendar

CHAPTER

31

The overwhelming need to get out of the house propelled me toward the front door. Once I was sufficiently bundled up, Mom came into the room. She didn't attempt to stop me or pull me to her. Instead, she gave me a sad smile.

"Don't go far, okay? The air has a bite in it tonight, and your dad saw a big bull moose down by the river earlier."

I nodded, then walked out into the frigid air. I'd lay money on this upcoming winter being even longer, darker, and colder than usual. Seemed fitting.

Keeping the moose in mind, I walked toward the river, but not all the way to it. I took my time, because it felt better to be outside, breathing fresh air. How could fate be so cruel? The text had plummeted me back into the same sorrowful spot I'd been in those days following Spencer's death. What had I done to deserve being dragged through this misery again, just when I'd begun to see bright patches in my life?

When I reached the Langleys' little split-log house at the end of the street, I turned back. I didn't want to venture into the more intense blackness closer to the river. Instead, I retraced my steps at much the same pace, even though my cheeks stung from the cold.

I was nearly at my house when I saw the bulky shape of someone walking in the opposite direction. Too late, I realized it was Jesse. I braced myself and tried to think of something plausible to say about my hasty departure from the rink and for the fact that he might not want to have anything to do with me anymore.

We stopped a few feet from each other. His face showed no expression, and that made my stomach queasy.

"Jesse . . . I'm sorry about earlier."

"Whatever."

His single-word response broke my heart even further. It seemed that no matter how broken, the heart could always shatter even more.

"Please let me explain."

He said nothing, just stood there with his hand wrapped around the handle of his bag.

I swallowed. "You probably think I've lost my mind, but I did get a text from Spencer. Only problem was, it was two months old. He had to have sent it the night before the crash, and I guess somehow a satellite has been hanging on to it for some unfathomable reason." That was the only sane explanation. It wasn't, after all, a message from the beyond.

Jesse didn't move or say anything, so I filled the uncomfortable silence by telling him about what the text had said and what it meant.

When I finished, Jesse finally took a couple of steps forward. "He's gone, Winter. You have to accept that."

"I know."

He didn't touch me, but his face held an intensity I'd never seen.

"I haven't pushed because of what happened to Spencer, but it should be obvious that I like you. I like how comfortable I am with you, how I never feel like I have to live up to some standard. Not to mention, you're beautiful." He paused, letting that statement sink in. "If you don't want to or can't be with me, tell me. If you do, you have to stop holding on to the past."

I'd known this already, but I was still stunned to hear the words spoken aloud. It made his feelings real, not just a product of my imagination.

"Think about it," he said, then passed me on his way to his house.

I stood there, letting his words ring in my ears, until even my thick Alaskan blood forced me inside.

The mountains in the distance were cloaked in jet black tonight, but I stared out my bedroom window in that direction anyway, thinking, until long after I heard Mom and Dad go to bed. When I glanced at Jesse's house, the pang in my heart made me press my hand to my chest. I'd hurt him— the last thing I'd wanted to do. Not so long ago, I would have said that was impossible.

But he did care. The words he'd spoken earlier proved it. And he was here, alive, wanting to be with me. He was right. I had to let Spencer go. Even though that thought hurt, I also acknowledged the thrill of excitement when I considered giving in to my attraction toward Jesse.

Despite the late hour, I texted Jesse. "R U AWAKE?"

After a few moments, a single "Y" popped onto my phone's display.

I called him, hoping I didn't wake his parents.

"Hey," he said. I wondered if he were lying in bed. That image made my skin warm all over. I might as well have been in Hawaii, not Alaska.

"Hey."

Silence hung between us. "You still there?" he asked.

I looked out the window, placing my hand on the cold pane. "I'm sorry . . . for everything."

The sound of rustling, distinctly bed-like rustling, met my ear. "I'm sorry if I was too mean earlier."

"No. You were right."

"So?"

I searched the hidden crevices of my brain for an appropriate response. "Do you still want to go to the Snow Ball? If you don't, I understand. I mean, I've—"

"Yes," he said. I thought I heard a slight laugh, too.

"I was babbling, wasn't I?"

"A little."

"Sorry." I pressed my forehead against the window and felt like banging some sense into myself.

"It's okay. It's kind of cute."

I smiled, stupidly fond of the way he said "cute."

"You really want to go?" I asked.

"As much as any guy wants to dress up and go to these things."

I did laugh then. "Wow, I'm overwhelmed by your excitement."

Even after we said good night, I sat next to the window and watched the inky night sky. Talking to Jesse had given me a sense of relief. Of hope. Like if I could just get past the Snow Ball, I could get past the lingering ties to Spencer.

I hoped I could keep my promise to myself to let go.

"When love beckons to you, follow him,
Though his ways are hard and steep."
—Kahlil Gibran, Quote-a-Day calendar

CHAPTER

32

I stared at the application in front of me and continued to flip the pen in my right hand over and over.

"You look like you're trying to figure out the meaning of the universe," Jesse said, next to my ear.

I jumped. I hadn't even heard him come up behind me. I'd retreated to the school library during my lunch break to fill out the application for the Fashion Institute of Design and Merchandising in Los Angeles. I'd already applied to the University of Alaska in Anchorage, but this . . . this was a step toward my long-held dream. I told myself I didn't have to fully commit to it unless I got in. I'd tackle that decision when (and if) I needed to.

Jesse slipped into the chair next to me and pointed at the admission form. "You know that won't complete itself, right?"

"Considering how long I've been staring at it, I was beginning to come to that conclusion."

Jesse grabbed the pen mid-twirl, positioned it in my hand, then guided my hand so the end of the pen pointed to the line next to the word "Name" on the application.

"You know you want this. Don't let anyone or anything stand in the way of going after it."

I looked into his eyes: those deep, dark, beautiful eyes. "How did you get to be so smart, Jesse Kerr?"

He gave me a crooked grin, one I'd seen often in the weeks since we'd agreed to go to the Snow Ball together. "I hang out with this smart girl who also happens to be kinda cute."

I smiled back and enjoyed the giddy feeling that was making my skin tingle. "That so?"

"It is." He wrapped his hand more fully around mine and squeezed.

He hadn't made a move to kiss me since the night of the text message from Spencer, but it seemed right. And I didn't get the feeling that it irritated him anymore. There was no doubt that the desire was still there, but I got the impression maybe he didn't want to push again. I thought he wanted to be sure I was really over Spencer before we did more than occasionally touch and exchange long glances across our classrooms.

I still thought of Spencer every day. Though it seemed a bit more of the darkness inside me drifted away as the days passed. I could finally focus more on the happy times we'd shared, and not his death.

I turned my hand over and squeezed Jesse's back. I liked this feeling of looking to the future instead of dwelling in the past, and I hoped it continued to get easier.

A shuffling noise from a table opposite the bookshelf caught my attention. When Patrice came into view, I stiffened for an attack. But, though she must have heard our conversation, she didn't even look at Jesse and me. Instead, she walked out of the library without a spiteful backward glance.

"Okay, odd," I said.

"Maybe she didn't notice us."

I gave him a "Seriously?" look.

He lifted his hands in surrender. "Okay, so that's not likely. I don't know—or care—what she's thinking."

In that moment, I felt as if I'd slipped through a crack into Bizarro Tundra again. Jesse and me going to the Snow Ball. Patrice studying alone in the library, then passing up an opportunity to be nasty. Was I dreaming?

Jesse used his forefinger to push several strands of hair behind my ear. "Don't think about her so hard. You'll give yourself a brain cramp." He pointed at the application again. "Focus on this instead."

I gave him a mock salute. "Yes, sir."

He rolled his eyes and stood. "See you in class."

I watched him as he left, appreciative of how he moved with a combination of ease and power. Even after he disappeared, I stared at the empty doorway. Again, Patrice's reaction puzzled me. When I thought about it, I realized she hadn't tortured me in weeks. In fact, we actually hadn't crossed paths that much. Was she avoiding me?

That should be a good thing, right? But I couldn't shake the feeling that when she'd left the library, she'd left a palpable trail of sadness in her wake.

CHAPTER

25

"What's past is prologue."
—*William Shakespeare,* The Tempest

CHAPTER

33

Mother Nature evidently wanted the world outside to match the decor inside the school's gym on the night of the Snow Ball. When I lowered my copy of *The Tempest*, I watched the real-life tempest blowing white and wild outside my bedroom window. Winter had arrived full force, Alaskan style, and well ahead of the calendar's designated "first day of winter." Thankfully, Jesse and I didn't have far to drive to the school.

I glanced at the clock, then rose from the chair. I walked to my full-length mirror and checked my dress one more time. The blue-and-white Regency-style gown—as well as the elbow-length white gloves and light-blue ribbon around the hair piled on top of my head—made me smile. I could almost hear Spencer's laughter at my homage to Jane Austen. I didn't know if Jesse would get the connection, but it didn't matter. I couldn't compare the two of them. They were different people who both meant a lot to me at different times in my life. Maybe I was a different person now, in some ways, than I'd been with Spencer.

I heard a knock on the door downstairs. Jesse. Before

going down to meet him, however, I indulged in one private moment of fantasy. I closed my eyes, positioned myself as if holding a partner's hand and shoulder, and danced a few steps around the room, imagining Spencer as my invisible date. We would have had a good time tonight. I swallowed the lump in my throat and told myself to focus on the evening as it was, not as it might have been.

I stopped spinning and faced the mirror again. I looked like a winter princess. Would Jesse prove to be my prince? I took a deep breath and pictured the look on his face as I came down the stairs, a moment straight out of a classic romance.

I had to laugh under my breath when I appeared at the top of the stairs to find no one waiting for me. The sound of dishes told me Mom was in the kitchen. Dad sat in his chair in front of the TV, and Jesse leaned on the back of the couch, both of them absorbed in the Canucks-Stars game.

I took a moment to appreciate the sight of Jesse in his black suit. I let the thought of my grand entrance fade away as I descended the stairs and walked across the living room. As I stepped up next to Jesse, I asked, "Who's winning?"

"The Can—"

His words died mid-answer, and his eyes widened as he looked at me. I found myself struggling for words, too. If I'd thought Jesse looked nice from the back, I was totally unprepared for the very nice things a dark suit did for him from the front. My heart beat faster than normal, and I felt a little weak. Cliché, but true.

"Oh, Winter, you look beautiful," Mom said from the side of the room.

Dad shook his head slowly in disbelief. "My baby, all grown up."

Jesse's brain seemed to reengage as he turned more fully toward me. "Your mom's right," he said low. "You look beautiful."

"Thanks." I fingered the dark lapel of his suit. "Much better than a hockey jersey."

"You know, I debated between the two."

"Come on, young and pretty people." Mom ushered us next to the mantel. "I want pictures before you go."

After a couple of minutes of photos, my parents allowed Jesse to help me into my coat.

"Be careful," Dad said. "It's wild out there tonight!"

When Jesse opened the door, the cold gusted inside as if hungry to find more warm air to consume. I huddled inside my thick hood as Jesse led me along the snow-covered driveway to the running SUV. Even with my long, down-filled coat, I was shivering by the time Jesse helped me into the passenger side. I watched as he hurried around the front to his own side.

Before he could slip into the SUV, a waft of warm air traveled around my shoulders and up my cheek. My breath caught for a moment. I knew the warmth wasn't a result of the SUV's heater. Spencer was here with me, no matter what anyone else thought. I smiled out into the night as I realized his presence felt comforting. Like a seal of approval.

When we arrived at the school, the sight of the gym's interior took my breath away. The Snow Ball committee really had outdone themselves. They'd transformed a place of sweat and squeaky sneakers into a fairy-tale winter wonderland.

Cotton batting sprinkled with silver glitter covered the refreshment table. It was mounded around the punch bowl to simulate a snowbank. Dozens of white and silver paper snowflakes hung on long strings from the rafters. Several white Christmas trees were grouped in one corner, like a snow-covered forest.

A DJ, made possible by the proceeds from the Halloween costume contest, already had tunes playing as we entered.

Everything was simply gorgeous, including Jesse. He pulled me into a dance, and my heart swelled. It wasn't the same type of deep feeling I'd harbored for Spencer all those years, but it was warm and sweet and held potential for something more.

I spotted Lindsay and Caleb as soon as they came in. The red sheath dress I'd made transformed my best friend into an exotic beauty, much like a movie star. I wasn't the only one who'd noticed.

Anja had cried the day before when she'd seen it, and I'd given her strict orders not to show it to Lindsay until right before she had to get ready. I didn't want Linds thinking too much, backing out of the dance or feeling like she owed me anything.

Watching her and Caleb and the intensity of the looks that passed between them, it was obvious they loved each other. If any couple left Tundra School and had a chance to stay together afterward, it was going to be those two. Lindsay had taken a huge step in that direction tonight by finally feeling confident enough to allow Caleb to see her meager, four-room home.

"Come on," I said as I took Jesse's hand and nearly dragged him toward Lindsay and Caleb. I heard the comments about how great Linds looked as I made my way toward her with a smile.

"You look gorgeous!" I grabbed her hands and held them out from her. "Like Miss America."

Caleb moved close to her, and his eyes sparkled with love. "Yeah, I have the most beautiful date here."

"Nothing against Lindsay, but I might argue with you," Jesse said from beside me as he placed his hand at the small of my back.

The compliment sent pleasure coursing through me. I looked up at him and smiled.

"Let's just say we're both smoking hot and leave it at that," Lindsay said. She leaned forward and hugged me, drawing my attention away from Jesse. "Thank you so much," she whispered in my ear. "I've never had anything so beautiful in my life."

"You deserve it. You and Caleb look so happy."

Lindsay squeezed my hand. "So do you."

I was happy. Part of me had dreaded this night for the past three months, but as I danced with Jesse and watched how Caleb made Lindsay's face light up, I realized I'd been wrong. Another piece of arctic cold that had breathed inside me since Spencer's death thawed and drifted away. I placed my cheek against Jesse's chest as we danced, focusing on his warmth and nothing else. Not on the remaining parts of my heart that still wished I could see Spencer just one more time.

I pushed that thought away and danced even when my feet started throbbing.

One of the late arrivals was Patrice Murray, and it wasn't a fashionably late entrance. She was dateless, and no gal-pal posse accompanied her, either. She entered the gym alone and headed straight for the refreshment table. For some reason, I couldn't stop watching her as Jesse and I continued to dance.

"What's wrong?" he asked.

"It's Patrice. She . . . she looks so sad." And despite everything, I found it saddened me in response.

Jesse looked at his old girlfriend. "Patrice Murray is not used to attending dances alone, even if it was her choice."

Something told me it was more than that, but I didn't voice the thought. I wondered why she'd decided to come alone, but I decided not to ruin my night by thinking about Patrice too much. Instead, I refocused my attention on my own *very* hot date.

After several songs and a glass of punch, I excused myself to the ladies' room. The one adjacent to the gym had a long line, so I made my way out into the empty corridor and headed for the restroom at the other end of the building. Expecting it to be as empty as the hallway, I gasped when I realized someone was standing inside.

Patrice looked just as startled by my arrival as I was by her. She stiffened and spun away, presenting me her back. It was obvious she'd been crying. I considered leaving her in private, but I didn't. I stood and listened as she tried to compose herself.

You're a good person, Winter Craig. Jesse's words came back to me. Time to live up to what he believed about me. I took a few steps forward.

"What's wrong, Patrice?" I asked tentatively.

"Nothing," she snapped.

I fought the urge to wash my hands of her once and for all. But I wanted to be the bigger person. As I decided that, the tone of her voice finally sank into my resistant brain. It was the sound of someone hurting.

I walked into an empty stall and pulled a wad of toilet paper from the roll. I offered it to Patrice, shoving it closer when she made no move to take it. When she finally wrapped her manicured fingers around it, I felt as if I'd won an enormous battle.

I wasn't surprised that she didn't thank me. That would likely be too big of a pill for her to swallow.

"Is this about me being here with Jesse?"

"What do you think?" Again with the sharpness.

"You know, the appropriate response to someone who is showing concern about you isn't to bite her head off."

Patrice heaved a long sigh. "Why are you in here?"

"The need to go to the bathroom might be the obvious answer."

She looked at me then, and I saw the redness rimming her eyes. "I mean when you saw I was in here, why did you stay?"

I crossed my gloved arms. "I don't really know. You make it difficult for someone to even think about caring about you."

Her laugh was totally devoid of humor. "That's what my mother says."

Something about the way she said it spoke of a very deep hurt. "Really? That's awful."

Shock registered on her face. But I couldn't imagine my mother saying something like that.

On the heels of her shock came embarrassment. Again, she turned away, causing the skirt of her sparkly pink fairy-tale dress to swish around her feet.

"I didn't mean to embarrass you," I said. "I just think . . ."

She glanced over her shoulder. "What?"

"This is going to sound all corny, school counselor–ish."

She continued to watch me. Despite the vicious lies Patrice had spread about me, I found myself trying to help her. She couldn't be more shocked than I was.

"What do you want, Patrice?"

Her eyebrows bunched.

"Is it really Jesse? Or is that what your mom wants you to have?"

Patrice turned and leaned against the sink. "Jesse told you about my parents, didn't he?"

"It came up."

She picked at the fabric of her skirt. "I don't know what I want. I've always just done what my parents said. Pathetic, huh?"

"More sad than pathetic."

We stood in silence for several seconds.

Patrice gestured toward her teary eyes. "This isn't because of Jesse. That was Mom's dream, that we'd end up married and be the king and queen of Tundra." She snorted. "As if I want to stay here for the rest of my life."

"So you do know one thing you want . . . to leave Tundra."

She looked at me for a moment. "I guess you're right. At least that's something."

"Have you told your parents?"

"What do you think? They're convinced I'm going to go to college but come back and be their next-door neighbor or something. Provide them with a herd of grandchildren whose lives they can run."

"Patrice." I waited until she lifted her gaze from the floor tiles. "You don't have to come back. We only have six months left, and then your life is your own. Between now and then, figure out what you want and go for it."

I watched as that knowledge sank in and part of her sadness lifted.

"I can't believe you're talking to me after how I've treated you."

I shrugged. "Maybe I hope you won't board the bitchy train again."

She stared at me so long and hard that I had to resist the urge to fidget.

"I see why Jesse likes you. Why Spencer did." She swallowed visibly, like she might have a lump in her throat. "I'm sorry about what I said that day at the craft fair. What happened to Spencer . . . it wasn't your fault."

I'd already accepted that, but it surprised me how much it meant to hear her say it.

Patrice pushed away from the sink. "I think I'm just going to go home. I look awful now anyway, and Mom's already ticked that I'm dateless. How much madder can she get?"

I wondered if that was the reason behind Patrice coming

to the dance alone—a bit of rebellion against her controlling mother.

She headed toward the door, her silver heels peeking out from beneath her dress. It seemed wrong for anyone to be so sad and lonely on the night of the Snow Ball. Fate had seen that I wasn't, but I feared the cost was Patrice's frame of mind.

"Patrice."

"Yeah?"

"Would you like to dance with Jesse before you go home?"

"I don't think he wants to dance with me."

"Tell him it's as friends, that I said it was okay."

She watched me as if she thought I might be messing with her before offering a small, shaky smile. "Thanks."

"You're welcome. Oh, and tell him I'll be back in a few minutes. I have to take care of something."

I used the restroom as the sound of Patrice's clicking heels faded down the hallway. When I left the restroom, I didn't turn back the way I'd come. With a deep breath, I headed for my locker. After I turned the familiar combination, I hesitated before opening the door.

I'd told Patrice to go after what she wanted. Time to take my own advice.

I opened the door and started slowly removing the smiling photos from inside, carefully peeling away the tape, taking long looks at those moments in time and sliding the photos into my handbag. When I took down a shot of Spencer and me grinning wide with our cheeks pressed together, I ran my thumb across his handsome face.

"Thank you." I thanked him for being my friend, for being my first love, and for understanding that I had to move on.

I gently placed the photo with the others and closed the clasp on my bag. I looked at the remaining photo in my locker—of Spencer, Lindsay, and me. Three best friends. I smiled at the image before closing the metal door and turning back toward the gym.

When I stepped inside, a song was ending, and Jesse was giving Patrice a hug. It didn't make me jealous, because I now knew how they both felt, and it wasn't how her parents wanted them to feel.

Patrice didn't hug me as she left. Despite our conversation, I doubted we'd ever be friends. And that was okay. I had Lindsay for that. And Jesse.

When I focused on him, I wanted to do much more than hug. I walked straight toward him.

"Hey. What—?"

I cut off his question by lifting on my toes and kissing him. It took only a moment for him to lean down and return the kiss. His firm-but-soft warm lips moved against mine, causing my whole body to react. My pulse thudded against my eardrums as I kissed him back.

When the kiss ended, I became intensely aware of the feel of Jesse's body pressed against mine. I managed to smile at him despite the fizzing in my brain.

"If I'd known that was going to happen, I would have danced with Patrice a lot sooner."

I laughed and pulled his lips to mine again.

"What is a youth? Impetuous fire.
What is a maid? Ice and desire."
—Glen Weston, "What Is a Youth?"
Quoted on a homemade valentine card from Jesse to
Winter, February, senior year

EPILOGUE

The wind screamed like a wild animal outside. Even for a girl who was Alaskan born and bred, it sounded freakishly cold.

"This makes the night of the Snow Ball look like spring break in Florida," Jesse said, from where he was looking out the front window of my living room. He leaned closer to the window. "I'm guessing the dark mass at your mailbox is Kerry delivering the mail."

"Living the postal service motto to the fullest," I said from my end of the couch, where I'd been doing my homework.

Jesse cut me off as I headed toward the coat closet. "I'll go get it."

I gave him a wicked smile and rubbed my hands together. "My evil plan has worked."

He tapped his temple. "I'll remember that."

I retreated to the couch and my thick afghan as Jesse slipped into his coat and stomped through the snow outside. I watched out the window as he raced across the yard to get our mail and his family's, then raced back in again.

When he blew in the front door, so much snow covered

his coat that he looked a bit like Frosty. I blinked dramatically at him. "My hero."

He discarded his coat, cap, and gloves and stalked toward me. "Your hero needs warming up."

I squealed as he jumped onto the couch and stuck his cold nose next to my neck.

"Oh my God, get away from me, icicle boy." I tried to squirm away from him, but he trapped me with his arms and legs.

"I might be persuaded to free you."

I knew what he wanted, but I played stupid. "And what's the price of freedom?"

He wiggled his eyebrows.

I laughed, then gave him the kiss he sought. Truth was, I liked our kisses just as much as he did. We hadn't talked long term, but the relationship we'd flowed into after the Snow Ball made us both happy. Neither of us seemed to want to mess with that happiness by posing big questions. For now, I wanted life to continue as simply as possible.

When he pulled away, I pushed him back and grabbed the mail he'd discarded on the coffee table. Bills, junk mail, doctor-type stuff for Dad . . .

I stared at the return address on the envelope in my hand.

"What is it?" Jesse asked, concern in his voice.

I looked up at him. "A letter from FIDM."

"Your acceptance letter." He sounded so sure.

"Or not." I stared at the words I'd wanted linked to my name for years. Fashion Institute of Design and Merchandising.

"Are you going to open it?"

"I don't know." I literally held the course of my future in my hand. It excited and frightened me at once.

Jesse turned my face toward his. "It's an acceptance letter. Your designs are too good for it not to be."

"But what if it is?"

Confusion tugged at his features. "That's not a problem, is it?"

"What if I can't hack it? What if I get homesick?" What if I couldn't break myself away for fear of losing Jesse, the way I had Spencer?

That question made me realize how very much he meant to me now.

He caressed my cheek. "Don't worry so much. You know they have planes between Anchorage and L.A., right? I even hear they fly between the two every day," he teased.

I swatted his shoulder. "Why do I put up with you?"

"Limited dating pool."

"There is that."

He'd lightened the mood enough that I was able to face the letter again. With a deep breath, I ripped it open and pulled out the single sheet of paper. I paused a few more seconds before I calmed myself enough to read.

"Dear Ms. Craig:

It is my pleasure to inform you of your acceptance. . . ."

I didn't get any farther. A huge smile stretched across my face as I jumped up and squealed. Then I plopped down next to Jesse and kissed him.

"I'm guessing you got in."

"Yes."

He wrapped his arm around my shoulders and pulled me close. "I'm happy for you."

"I'm so excited I feel like I might be sick!"

"Make you a deal. If you get sick when you arrive in California, I promise to lose my cookies before my first game at UAA."

"Wish I could see you play there."

"I promise to have videos made and sent to you. All the girls at your school will be jealous."

I pulled back. "They might think you're too cocky for you own good."

He shrugged and gave me another of those adorable crooked smiles. "It's a chance I'm willing to take."

I was going to miss him. And Lindsay. And Caleb. They were all going to school at the University of Alaska Anchorage, just like my sisters.

He nestled me into the crook of his arm again, and I placed my head against his chest. "Things will work out," he said. "Hey, I'm already envisioning spring break in So Cal. I might even let Caleb and Lindsay tag along."

"That sounds like fun."

"Yes, bikinis as far as the eye can see."

I punched him in the side. He feigned injury, then wrestled me halfway onto his lap so I was facing him. After a slow, sweet kiss, he looked a little more serious.

"One day at a time, remember?"

The phrase I'd used the night of the Snow Ball, when we'd sat in my living room and talked all night about Spencer, and how I could only let Jesse into my life a little more one day at a time. "But it's easier when the people are in the same state," I said.

"It doesn't have to be easy to be worth it."

I thought I might love him. No, I knew I did. But I had to take the chance of going after my dream. I owed that to Spencer who hadn't gotten to live his.

I owed it to myself.

"Besides," Jesse said, "I'm not that easily gotten rid of. When you walk down the red carpet at the Oscars, you'll need a hot date."

"Guess I better start looking when I get there, huh?"

Jesse wrapped his arms around me and pulled me close. "Only if you think you have to."

Peace and happiness settled side by side inside my heart, a heart no longer cold and empty but filled with possibilities.

ACKNOWLEDGMENTS

Special thanks to Monica McCabe, for her tales of her time in Alaska and her willingness to let me pick her brain for the price of a Longhorn Steakhouse lunch.